KEY OF DESTINY

KEY OF DESTINY

By Jerry Garcia

Self-Published with help by
MIDNIGHT EXPRESS BOOKS

BOOK TITLE

Self-Published with help by
MIDNIGHT EXPRESS BOOKS
POBox 69
Berryville AR 72616
(870) 210-3772
MEBooks1@yahoo.com

KEY OF DESTINY

By Jerry Garcia

Dedicated to my daughter Brianna Garcia

Who has always occupied

her own sacred chamber

within my heart.

ACKNOWLEDGEMENTS

I would like to thank Paul Drummond, Heath Ransom, Jose Herrera, Elias Custodio and Roy Rojas for their support and encouragement throughout the writing of this book.

And a special thanks to Earl Grove for his contribution of the cover art.

Thank you all!

Key of Destiny

2

Zacharias awoke shivering, he had kicked off his blankets while having a bad dream, or at least he thought it was a bad dream, he couldn't remember much of it, except that a brute of a man on a horse was chasing him, **este demonio** *(this demon)* carried a saber at his waist side, it was like a half sword with an ivory hilt, the menacing blade was about three inches wide and every bit of two and a half feet long.

Fully awake now, he scrambled to retrieve his blankets encasing himself up in them, it was in this fetal position lying on his side, that he caught sight of his bed that his father had started to assemble the day before, it was of no use yet, because the mattress and box spring were in the u-haul that was supposed to arrive sometime this morning.

He never realized before how much of a comfort it was to have a bed, but after being exposed to the stone floor for a second night in a row, not being able to escape the chill of the stone throughout the entire night, he promised himself that he would never take it for granted again.

All this was forgotten as quickly as he realized today was Saturday; yesterday his **mami** *(mother)* had enrolled him at Lincoln Elementary School here in Denver Colorado.

The past week had seemed like a dream to him, his father Alejandro, mother Appolonia and little sister Brianna had just moved here two days ago from San Antonio **Tejas** *(Texas)*, to this stone mansion that his **Bis-Abuelo** *(great grandfather)*, Zacharias **puños de pierda** *(hands of stone)* Garcia, had built for his family at the turn of the century.

His Abuelo had been a captain in Pancho Villas Revolutionary Army, he had died a heroes death at the battle over the city of Juarez Mexico, Because of his untimely death, he had failed to move his family north to Colorado, so for the last three generations they had continued to live in San Antonio, his father Alejandro, having inherited the place, had decided it was time to fulfill his Grandfather's wishes.

Zacharias looked out the window and noticed the stars were starting to fade, the sun wasn't up yet, but it wouldn't be long, more to escape the chill of the stone floor than anything else, he got out from underneath his blankets, even though it was very early, he knew his **mami** *(mother)* would already be up serving his **papi** *(father)* **cafesito con leche** *(coffee with cream)*.

He put on his slippers and dashed to the restroom, washed his hands, splashed some water on his face and snagged up his robe on the way out the door.

As he approached the foot of the stairs, he caught the wonderful aroma of the tortillas his mami was cooking on the **comal** *(a cast iron hot-plate for cooking tortillas)*.

He ran down the stairs and into the kitchen and said, "**Buenos dias mami**" *(Good day mother)* then, "**Buenos dias papi.**" *(Good day father)*

His mother replied, "**Buenos dias mijito**'" *(Good day my beloved son)*, you're up awful early this morning."

His father then boomed, "**Buenos dias hijo.** *(Good day my son)*, **Como amaneciste, Bravo-o-Contento?**" *(How did you awaken,* *angry or content?)* .

Zacharias answered, "Contento, but a little cold."

His papi smiled and said, "Then it shall be a good day!"

His mami brought him some hot chocolate and a fresh tortilla straight from the comal, he seized it and immediately spread butter over it, the butter melted away into the tortilla instantly, he rolled it up into a burrito shape and started to devour it, God how he enjoyed **tortillas con mantequilla**, *(tortillas with butter)* early in the morning, come to think of it, anytime of the day they were pretty good!

"What do you want for breakfast mijito ?" asked his mami.

Zacharias answered, "Eggs, a slice of ham, beans and a little **chilito** *(homemade salsa)* **porfavor mami**" *(please mother).*

"**Ese es el hijo de su padre**," *(that's his father's son)* said his mami.

His papi beamed proudly and said, "That'll help you grow strong, and the chilito will put hair on your chest!"

Zacharias wasn't sure whether what his **papi** said about the chilito was true or not, but he put a little on every meal just in case.

"And what do you remind yourself every morning before

breakfast," Chided his papi.

Zacharias sat up straight and said, "**Siempre a tratar a la gente con respeto, si yo espero que mi respeten a mi.**" (*always treat people with respect, if I in turn wish to be respected*)

"And what else," urged his papi.

"Oh yeah, "**Y siempre de tratar de ayudar las personas que no se puedan ayudar ellos mismos!**"(*and always try and help those who cannot help themselves.*)

"**Muy bien hijo!**" (*very good son.*) said his papi.

His father was an attorney with the A.C.L.U. and was very adamant about fighting the good fight, as he liked to say, meaning, he liked to champion the causes of the little man against big business or the government, always trying to win equal rights for the oppressed and under privileged, in Zacharias' eyes, his father was a hero larger than life, and he loved and respected him more than anyone else on earth.

"**Mijo** (*my son*), everything that belongs in your room arrives today, I'll have everything hauled up to your room by tonight, first thing tomorrow morning, I expect you to get everything squared away, that's your responsibility, are we understood?"

"**Si papi,**" (*yes father*) said Zacharias. Today however, is yours to do with what you wish, get acquainted with the place, just stay out of your mother's way; she has a lot to do," said his papi.

"Si papi," said Zacharias, he couldn't wait, he wanted to go explore, so immediately after breakfast he excused himself and ran up the stairs.

He was in his room getting dressed when he heard his father calling him.

"Zacharias"

He turned around but no one was there, he ran out of his room to the foot of the stairs, and still didn't see anyone. He yelled out "papi," but no one answered, he shrugged it off and returned to his room, as he was walking by his window, he saw his father and mother removing stuff from the trailer they had pulled behind his father's pickup truck, they were way across the lawn, yet who had called his name? He could have sworn it was his father's voice. At that very instant he remembered **El Demonio** (*the demon*) he had dreamt about!

Starting from the point of the hair on his head then continuing all the way down his entire body, he felt a damp chill wash over him, when he looked out the window again, he noticed a small girl about his age staring over from the lawn across the street, he felt a little embarrassed because he had been standing so stiff and rigid, he suspected that she had seen the frightened look on his face, he immediately tried to appear relaxed and at ease, but it was too late, she had put her hands to her face and was giggling, she then turned and ran away up the driveway.

He thought she almost looked familiar, but that was crazy, he didn't know anyone in this neighborhood yet.

When he turned away from the window, the first thing he saw was his cowboy boots sticking up out of a box, that's when he knew he would begin his exploration outside first.

As he sat on the floor putting them on, he remembered there were lots of hedges, blackberry plants, brambles,, and all kinds of cool looking stuff he had seen out of one of the back room windows yesterday, He had also seen some discarded boards, planks and other junk he could probably use to build some kinda fort, or if his papi would help, maybe even a tree house, but that wouldn't be for a while yet, because he knew it would take his papi a few days to get their mansion in order first, before he would have time to help him with a tree house.

But that didn't mean he couldn't go out today and see if there was anything out there that was useable.

As he went out his bedroom door, the incipient fear he had experienced was all but forgotten.

CHAPTER TWO

As Zacharias began descending the stone steps after exiting the front door of the mansion, he caught sight of the girl again, she was still across the street, but this time there was a boy with her, she waved, so Zacharias waved back.

Then they both started across the street towards him, as they approached, it finally hit him where he remembered her from, she was in his classroom at school, he had seen her there yesterday.

"Hi, your name is Zachary, isn't it?"

Zacharias replied, "Yeah."

"I'm Julie, I saw you in school yesterday, we're in the same classroom, and this is my friend Blackie, we live across the street."

"I'm William Blackwood Morgan, but everybody calls me Blackie."

"I'm Zacharias Garcia, but you can call me Zach if it's easier."

Blackie tried it, "Zachaaaarrrriiiuuusss; yeah I think I'd rather call you Zach if it's okay."

"Sure it is," replied Zacharias with a smile on his face.

"This is where you're gonna live? No one's ever lived here before, that I know of," said Julie.

Blackie interjected, "My Great Grandfather had our house built back in 1917, and legend has it, that no one's lived in your mansion, since then anyway, but if you really want to know, I'm sure we could find something in the city archives."

Staring at Blackie, Julie said, "I'm surprised you don't know already!," then looking over at Zachary she says, "He's kind of a genius."

Blackie's face reddened a little as he spat out "I am not!"

10

"Well, you're definitely a bookworm anyway," retorted, Julie.

"Well you make it sound as if it's bad to want to learn stuff," he shot back.

"I never said it was bad to wanna learn stuff," said Julie.

Meanwhile, Zacharias was staring at these two with a smile on his face, because he knew he was going to like these two characters.

He had to interrupt them saying, "Hey. Hey. I already know no one's ever lived here before."

"You do?" asked Julie.

"Sure, my **Bisabuelo** (*great grandfather*) Zacharias Garcia, I was named after him, built it; I'm not sure exactly what year, but it was in the early nineteen hundreds. After he built it, he had to go back to Mexico because of the Revolution; he was one of Pancho Villas' most trusted **capitanes** (*captains*)."

Julie said, "Pancho who?"

"Pancho Villa," said Zacharias.

Julie said, "Who's that?"

Blackie interjected saying, "Pancho Villa and Emiliano Zapata, were the two most recognized generals in the Mexican Revolutionary

Army."

"Exactly!, said Zacharias, anyway, he had to go back to Mexico where he died a hero's death at the battle over the city of Juarez Mexico, he was known as, **púnos De Pierda** (*fists of stone*) because he was known for beating two and three men at a time with his bare fists."

Both Julie and Blackie simultaneously said, "Really?"

"Yeah, he was one of Pancho Villas' bravest Capitanes," said Zacharias beaming with pride.

Anyway, after he died, his family, my ancestors, stayed in San Antonio, Tejas; my mami told me that she suspects that they didn't have enough money to make the move, times were extremely rough back then, a lot of folks didn't even have enough to eat, but she says the main reason they didn't move here was because they had lost the head of the family, so there was no one to lead them to Colorado, that's why it's been empty ever since it was built, we're the first ones to live in it."

"Interesting," muttered Blackie.

Looking up at the mansion Julie said, "It must be five times as big as our house."

"More like ten times," corrected Blackie.

"You guys must be rich!" exclaimed Julie.

"We're not rich!" blurted Zacharias. "I mean we're not poor, but I don't think we're rich," for the first time feeling a little self-conscience around his new friends.

Blackie said, "Having been built around the turn of the century, it couldn't have been equipped with electricity, having to convert now I'm sure will cost a small fortune, not to mention repairs and a hundred other things that are certain to crop up.

Zacharias had never had to think of such things, in truth he never even considered whether his parents had or didn't have enough money, but now that he thought about it, he remembered hearing his mami telling his papi when they were back in San Antonio, 'Alejandro, what are we going to do with a great mansion in Colorado that we can't even afford to live in, and that maybe he should consider selling it, but that was as far as she'd gotten, because his papi had fixed her with a cold stare saying "**Nunca Vendere la Casa de mi abuelo, que hizo con sus propias manos y nunca me Vuelvas mencionar que lo haga otra Vez!**" (*I will never sell the home that my grandfather built with his bare hands, and never ask me to do so again*). So, that was the end of that, it was never brought up again.

"How many rooms does it have?" asked Julie bringing Zacharias out of his reverie.

"Oh, Uh...my papi said it's supposed to have twenty eight bedrooms and eleven bathrooms."

"ELEVEN BATHROOMS!" exclaimed Julie. "Why would you need eleven bathrooms?"

"I don't think that we're going to use them all," said Zacharias. "How many people are going to live here with you?" asked Julie.

"Just me, my mami and papi, and my little sister; she's three years old."

"Is that your mom and dad over there by the pickup truck?" asked Julie.

"Yeah, said Zacharias, "that's them."

"I thought so," said Julie. "I saw them out there earlier this morning when I saw you up in the window, but then who was that other man that was with you?"

"There wasn't anyone with me earlier when I saw you, I was in my bedroom by myself."

Julie said, "No you weren't! I saw that man pouring a pitcher of water or something over your head; that's why I was laughing."

Zacharias remembered the damp chill that had started at his head and had covered his entire body earlier that morning. At the time, it had felt as if someone had poured a pitcher of liquid over him. Suddenly and unexpectedly, he felt the rise of goose bumps all over his body. He felt frozen stiff as if he were one of the many slabs of beef he remembered seeing suspended from the hooks in the ceiling, in the freezer rooms of his uncle's slaughterhouse back in San Antonio.

Julie seeing Zacharias' terror stricken face said, "What's wrong Zachary?"

Zacharias, out of fear and disbelief, lashed out at her saying, "You're llllyyying!"

"No, I'm not," whimpered Julie.

But before she could continue Zacharias said, "I thought you wanted to be my friend but all you wanna do is make stuff up to try and scare me."

Julie was in tears, and in between sobs, she was trying to say that she hadn't made it up.

Blackie intervened saying, "Calm down Zach, I've know Julie a long time, she wouldn't make something like that up."

Zacharias, still frightened, started to calm down, accepting the realization that she might have indeed seen something, the more he considered what she had said, the more convincing it sounded.

15

Blackie turned around and put his arm around Julie trying to get her to stop crying as he led her across the lawn towards her house.

Zacharias, realizing that he had acted like a total jerk, ran after them saying, "Julie, Blackie, wait! Please wait a minute."

Julie stopped walking jerking Blackie to a halt alongside her.

Zacharias came around in front of them and said, "I'm really sorry Julie, I had no right to yell at you and I shouldn't have said you were lying."

Seeing the tears in her eyes brought up a lump in his throat, and his eyes started to sting, he had to look away for a moment to regain his resolve and to catch his breath; suddenly like a thundering waterfall he heard his papi's voice in his ears saying "**Hombres nunca lloran delante de una mujer.**" (*men never cry in front of a women*). It required every ounce of his dignity not to do so. He turned back around to face her, dropped to one knee, took her hand in his saying "I guess I..." Zacharias stuttering continued, "I guess I just got a little scared, and...and I'm just really sorry, and I hope you'll accept my apology."

Julie flushed as she moved her head up and down and started to wipe away her tears.

Blackie reached out grabbing Zach by the shoulder and helped him up saying, "Well done ole' chap! Couldn't have done that better myself."

Julie looked at Zachary and said, "I'm sorry too, if I scared you; I really didn't mean too."

"Awe, it's all right. I wasn't really scared," said Zacharias jutting out his chin hoping that this would make him appear as if he had not been frightened at all.

Here Blackie interjected saying, "I'm still confused as to what you did or didn't see?" Looking from Julie to Zach he said, "You stated that you were alone in your room, is that correct?"

Zacharias said, "I was alone, I think."

"And Julie, you said, that you saw a person up there with him, correct?"

"Well, I think there was," said Julie.

"Well then, what was it exactly that you saw?" asked Blackie.

"Well," said Julie. "Zachary was standing up in front of the window and it looked like there was a man standing behind him pouring a pitcher of, I don't know what, over Zachary's head."

"What did he look like?" asked Blackie.

Julie thought for a moment then said, "I don't really know, all I could see was an outline of a man with a hat on."

"What kind of hat," asked Zacharias.

"A big hat, like Mexican people wear," she said.

"You mean a **Sombrero** (*a Mexican hat*)," exclaimed Blackie.

"Yeah, a sombrero," said Julie. "At least that's what it looked like."

"Does this mean anything to you, Zach?" asked Blackie.

Zacharias said, "Well, yes and no...but....," then he proceeded to tell them about his dream, the voice he thought he had heard, the damp chill...in short, everything that he had experienced. When he was done, he said, "So what do you guys think? Do you think our mansion is haunted?"

Blackie said, "Let's not jump to conclusions, what we need is more information or clues of some sort, if the place is haunted, and I'm not saying it is mind you, it certainly wouldn't be the first time some such thing has occurred.

I believe what we need is further investigation."

Julie said, "ARE YOU SAYING YOU WANNA GO CHASING

AFTER A GHOST?? IS THAT WHAT YOU'RE SAYING? ARE YOU OUTTA YOUR FREAKING MIND, WILLIAM BLACKWOOD MORGAN???"

"No, I don't think so," said Blackie. "But I have read several books on spirits, lost souls, ghouls, and other phenomenon. Now what we need to keep in mind is most spirits, ghosts, lost souls or whatever term you wish to identify them with, contrary to popular belief, are not evil, although there are exceptions, but for the most part, most spirits, I prefer this terminology, are simply caught between worlds, because they have something yet to achieve or rid their burden of, once this is accomplished, the soul of the spirit is released, free to continue its journey to the next world and its final resting place, sometimes they're in need of outside intervention; a helping hand so to speak to help them with their deed."

"YOU'VE TOTALLY LOST IT THIS TIME, BLACKWOOD!" said Julie.

Zacharias said, "We can tell my parents that…"

Before he could finish, Blackie interrupted saying, "Tell them what exactly? That Julie *thinks* she saw someone! Or, that you *think* you heard someone! We need facts, ole' chap!"

"As crazy as it sounds, I don't see where I have a choice, it's either that, or wait in fear until it decides to come looking for me," said

19

Zacharias.

"GREAT! NOW I GOTTA LIVE NEXT TO TWO LUNATICS," exclaimed Julie.

"What do you mean YOU don't have a choice," asked Blackie. "You don't think I'm gonna let you go have all the fun yourself do you?"

Zacharias said, "What I meant is, I wouldn't expect you to help me. I mean, you did say yourself that it could be dangerous."

"So could crossing the street if you're not careful," said Blackie.

"Well, having someone else along would probably be safer, so what kinda clues exactly are we going to be looking for?" asked Zacharias.

Blackie replied, "From what I understand, most spirits have a certain area or room, that they hold as their sacred chamber, although they may roam the entire mansion, they always return to their sacred chamber, because if they stay gone for too long, their spirit begins to weaken, or so it's said, so if we can locate its sacred chamber, that would most definitely be the place we would need to search for clues."

Zacharias was considering what Blackie said. Although he wasn't convinced that his house was haunted, he had to admit it warranted further investigation. And Blackie did seem to know an awful lot about spirits, so he turned to Julie and said, "It's 9:15am. If we're not back by noon, tell my parents..."

Julie said, "You think I'm going to let you two go off by yourselves? ARE YOU BONKERS? Somebody's gotta look after you two!"

"But I thought you said..."

"Never mind what I said Zachary! We're all going and that's final!"

Blackie looked over at Zach shrugged and said, "Once she's made up her mind, you won't talk her out of it."

And it was like this, that all three kids' fate was thrust together as one. Not aware of the perils that lay ahead, all three, Zacharias, Blackie, and Julie, began an adventure, that not even in their wildest imaginations would they have thought possible.

Key of Destiny

CHAPTER THREE

"Where do you guys think we should start looking?" asked Zacharias.

Blackie replied, "Wherever we start, we'll need a flashlight, remember, there's no electricity, some of the rooms are bound to be pretty dark."

Julie said, "Is there anything else that we should take?"

Blackie seamed to ponder this for a moment, and then said, "It's times like these, that I wish I didn't have allergic reactions to dog hair."

Julie said, "What do you mean at times like these? Dog what? WHAT IN TARNATIONS ARE YOU BLABBERING ABOUT BLACKWOOD!"

Blackie said, "Well, if I recall correctly, I believe I read someplace, that animals have what's called a heightened sense perception. It's widely believed that they have a specialized body sense organ structure that receives, or is sensitive to, internal and external stimuli."

"In English, Blackwood!" said Julie.

Blackie said, "There are those who believe that animals can pick up on spirits, and or other phenomenon, way before humans can, all right!"

Having heard this, a grin shown on Zacharias' face as he remembered his pet **Gallo** (*rooster*), Pepé. But that didn't last long; his smile turned into a concentrated frown as he recalled in his mind's eye his last encounter with Pepé. It was back in San Antonio the day his parents told him that they would be moving to Denver, Colorado. He was upset because he didn't want to move. All his life he had grown up with his cousins and now he would be leaving them behind.

It was in this state of mind that he exited the back door of the house.

He normally avoided going out at this hour, this being the hottest time of the day; for to do so, in mid July, was considered by some to be an act of insanity. But he was angry and confused; feeling instantly rebellious. He told himself he wouldn't go, and they couldn't make him!

He was so channeled into his anguish, that his innate defenses were temporarily dis-engaged. As he planted his foot on the last step, it was as if he had frozen in time, he sensed danger, but before all of this culminated into a conscious thought, it was too late.

Peripherally, he saw a flash of red; Pepé, his pet Gallo, was in mid-flight and zeroed in on his shoulder. It was not so much the blow, but the maniacal whipping of wings that knocked him off his feet. In a rage, Zacharias flayed wantonly at Pepé causing him to retreat forthwith. As Zacharias stood up and began dusting himself off, he spied Pepé spreading his wings and strutting in front of his coop.

Instantly, his anger subsided for he knew, that if Pepés attack had been mal-intended, he would have been spilling blood at this point, but still as a safeguard against future attacks.

He made sure Pepé overheard him say, "**dicé mi mami que Gallo con arroz -y- chilito, es unos de los platos mas sabrosos, en todo Mexico!**" (*My mother says rooster with rice and salsa, is one of the* *most sought after dishes, in all of Mexico!*) But inside, Zacharias couldn't help but feel proud of Pepé's stealth, for even though he was a grandpa in rooster age, he still displayed a warrior's heart and cunning.

Pepé, in his youth, was one of the most feared **Gallo Guerreros** (*fighting cocks*) of his time, and the entire **Barrio** (*neighborhood*) still paid homage by offering him corn on his daily walks with Zacharias.

As Zacharias came out of his reverie, Julie had hold of his arm saying, "Zachary, are you okay?"

Zacharias said, "Oh, Uh...yeah. Hey Blackie, can any animal have that extra sensory stuff you were talking about?"

Blackie said, "From what I've read, that seems to be the general consensus."

Zacharias said, "Well then we can take Pepé with us!"

Both Blackie and Julie simultaneously said, "Who's Pepieee?"

Zacharias said, "Not Pepieee, Pepé; my **Gallo**; you know, rooster."

Julie said, "You have a rooster?"

Zacharias' back stiffened up and his jaw jutted out, you could see the pride in his mannerisms alone, "Pepé was the bravest and most feared Gallo in my whole Barrio, when he was younger. He's old now, so he doesn't fight anymore, but he's still brave, and smart too!"

Julie said, "He won't attack us, will he?"

Zacharias said, "He was raised to fight other Gallos so he doesn't attack people. Well, he almost never attacks people. There were these two brothers back home, Ramon and Freddy. They were throwing rocks at him once, and Pepé chased them all the way home. They were lucky they got indoors before Pepé got to them. But as long as you don't throw rocks at him, he'll like you."

"You can be assured I won't be throwing anything at him," said Blackie.

"Me neither," said Julie. "I want him to like me."

Before Zacharias could answer, his papi was coming around the side of the house; he caught sight of them and said, "Mijo I see you've already made some new friends."

Zacharias replied, "Papi, this is Blackie and Julie; they both live across the street."

Blackie reached out his hand and said, "I'm William Blackwood Morgan, but it's quite a mouthful, so most people tend to call me Blackie, sir."

Alejandro said, "Well then, Blackie it is young man."

Then he turned to Julie and said, "And what might be your name young lady?"

"Julie O'Malley. It's nice to meet you, Mr. Garcia," answered Julie.

"The pleasure is all mine, I assure you madam," he said, as he bowed like a Spanish Monarch.

Julie giggled.

Zacharias said, "Papi where's Pepé? I haven't seen or heard him all morning."

Alejandro said, "that's because I thought it might get too cold for him if we left him outside overnight. This is a large change in climate for him, so I set up his coop in one of the big rooms down stairs at the back end of the mansion; that's why you haven't heard him. Why don't you, Blackie and Julie take him down some feed and fresh water and let him outta his coop?"

"Okay, papi," said Zacharias. We can take him with us to go explore."

Alejandro said, "I haven't had a chance to go through each and every room yet, but the place seems safe enough, so I'll trust you to use your best judgment. I better get going, I've got a hundred things to do, you have fun, but be careful."

"Si, papi," said Zacharias.

"We will," echoed Blackie and Julie as they tramped off around the corner.

Key of Destiny

CHAPTER FOUR

As they entered the side door that lead into the kitchen, Zacharias said, "I think I remember seeing a flashlight in one of the boxes we put in here yesterday. Hey can one of you put some of that feed right there into a bowl for Pepé?"

"Yeah, I'll do it," said Julie.

She filled a plastic bowl with feed and fetched a second bowl for water. She turned around; then turned around again in the opposite direction. She didn't see a sink anywhere. She said, "Hey Zachary, where's the sink?"

Zacharias looked up from the box he had been digging in and said, "We don't have any sinks, there's a spigot back around that corner; that's where we get our water from."

"Oh, okay," said Julie.

She went around the corner and into a corridor of some sort, instantly she felt a chill over her body. It was at least fifteen degrees cooler in this room and the ceilings were taller, at least thirty feet high or so she thought; it was too dark in there for her to be certain. Impulsively, her hand went up in search of a light switch, but all she encountered was damp cobblestone. Startled, she jerked her hand away, then giggled to herself saying, "What the heck am I doing, there's not even a sink in this place, and I'm looking for a light switch. Pull it together Jewels," she told herself.

Then she heard the sound of dripping water; it seemed to be coming from the far end of the corridor. She took a few tentative steps in that direction squinting her eyes.

The first thing that came into focus were three wooden pails, they were lined up on the far wall, to the left was an iron grid imbedded into the floor, and about three feet above that was the spigot, it protruded about eight inches from the wall, then elbowed so that it pointed directly down into the iron grid, the grid itself was a three foot by four foot grid.

32

As she neared, she attempted to peer down into it, but it was too dark and deep for her to see anything, instinctively, she knew it was a long way down, her stomach contracted and she began to feel regret for having volunteered to come and get the stupid water, she placed her right foot on the grid applying pressure making sure it would hold her, to her relief it had no weakness, whomever had constructed it had built it solid and true, she thanked her god for small miracles.

The spigot had an extremely large handle which was obviously meant to be pulled downward, she held the bowl with her left hand approximately three inches away and directly underneath the spigot, she then pulled the handle down wide open.

For a second nothing happened, then she began to hear the straining and creaking of pipes that seemed to her were coming from the very bowels of the mansion itself.

The water came thundering out with such force, it tore the bowl out of her hands and sent it skipping down the corridor.

At the moment the water had made contact with the bowl, she shrieked and had taken a step backwards or so she thought, the next thing she knew, was that she was flat on her rear end looking up at Zacharias and Blackie as they came running into the corridor showering her in a beam of light.

Zacharias grabbed her arm and was helping her up saying

something she couldn't quite hear, then he reached over and shut off the water.

He turned to her and said, "Are you okay Julie, are you hurt?" Blackie had a hold of her other arm and was also asking if she was okay.

She had been frightened and had panicked, but now all she was feeling was embarrassed, "let go of me, I'm okay," she heard herself say, as she jerked free of them.... "If it wasn"t for that *thing*, for that fire hydrant *thing* you call a spigot!!!"

Zacharias interrupted saying, "It's my fault Julie, I'm sorry, I shouldn't have sent you in here alone, I wasn't thinking, I should have known better, are you sure you're okay."

Julie having collected her wits about her, heard the sincerity in Zacharias' voice, she then said, "Awe, I'm all right, I just got a little spooked that's all, look I hardly got wet, it just caught me by surprise, that water comes out awful fast you know."

Zacharias said, "Yeah, I should have told you, see, you have to put one of these buckets here underneath the spigot first, and then turn the lever half-way only, or you'll get...., well I guess you already know what'll happen."

Julie said, "Yeah no kidding!"

Zacharias continued, "Then we use this ladle right here to scoop out the water."

Blackie said, "It's fortunate this occurred now."

Julie said, "FORTUNATE? WHAT'S FORTUNATE ABOUT ME GETTING KNOCKED ON MY REAR END?"

Blackie, taking a step backwards said, "It's fortunate in the sense that this incident should serve as an example of what could happen if we don't stick together, sure you just got knocked on your tush this time, but who knows next time, all I'm saying is to minimize risk, I believe it would be prudent to stick together at all times, I'm not saying there's anything to be frightened of, it's just simply a safety precaution."

Hearing this Zacharias said, "hey guys, maybe this isn't such a hot idea, I mean there probably isn't anything to go looking for anyway, and I know my papi would be really upset if anyone was to get hurt, maybe we should just forget about it." Julie exclaimed, "I JUST STUMBLED. GEEEZ. LET IT GO!"

Blackie turned to Zacharias and said, "Hey ole' chap, I understand your concern, but we're all in this now, and to quote from one of the epic works of Dumas, 'it's all for one, and one for all; am I right?"

"YOU'RE DARN TOOTIN!" said Julie.

Blackie continued, "Zach, you may be right, there may not be anything to search for, and that'll be okay, but if there is, maybe we could help, or at least figure out what it wants, the possibilities are endless; anyway, the one thing I do know, is that there's safety in numbers, and who knows, this could turn out to be hero stuff, and I'm certainly not going to let chance pass me by."

"Yeah, me neither!" said Julie.

"Sounds like you've been out-voted," said Blackie.

Zacharias said, "Nothing I can say is going to change your minds?"

Blackie and Julie both piped in at the same time, "Nope!"

Blackie looked over at Julie and said, "Come on Julie; put your hand on top of mine. All for one, and one for all."

Julie reached out placing her palm flat over the top of Blackie's hand, they both waited for Zacharias, he stared at both of them for a moment, then said, "all right we go together."

As he placed his palm flat onto Blackie, and Julie's outstretched hands, they all said in unison, "all for one, and one for all!"

CHAPTER FIVE

As they approached the rear door from the outside, Julie was the first one to reach it, she turned the knob and pushed, nothing happened, "I think it's locked," said Julie

Zacharias sat down the bowl of water and said, "Here let me try."

As Blackie was setting down the chicken feed he was carrying, he said, "that door appears to be solid oak, at least four inches thick; here, allow me to give you a hand ole' chap." Zacharias turned the knob and they both pushed with their hands, it seemed to budge a little but still didn't open.

Blackie said, "Okay, let's put our shoulders into it, and on the count of three, we push with all our might.... ready?"

"Okay," said Zacharias. "One, two, three Push."

Once it gave, it burst open full swing sending Zacharias to his knees, and Blackie right over the top of him flattening him out like a welcome mat.

Before Zacharias had the time to admonish Blackie for landing on him, they all three simultaneously heard the maniacal whipping of wings and cries of battle coming from Pepé in the next room.

Blackie shot up like a cat, showing remarkable agility for a boy of his mirth, he was up and running shoulder to shoulder with Zacharias, and Julie was nipping at their heels as they entered the next room, they came to screeching halt just inside, the room was bare except for Pepés coop in the far corner, he was airborne, claws extended in front of him in attack formation, slamming into one side and then the other of his cage, at this very instant all three felt a distinct breeze rush past them leaving an odor of tobacco and something else.

Zacharias screamed, "**calmaté Pepé, porfavor calmate', te vas a lastimar**" (*settle down, please settle down, you're going to hurt yourself*), as he dropped to his knees in front of the coop door and swung it open. Pepé shot out like a bullet flying around the room with reckless abandon.

Blackie yelled out, "HIT THE DECK!" as he dove for the floor.

Julie was flat on her stomach with her arms around her head half a second later.

Zacharias was chasing Pepé around the room saying,

"It's okay, Pepé. It's okay. What's wrong with you?"

Pepé landed in the far corner half strutting, half hopping, with his wings extended still on the defensive, but beginning to calm down.

Zacharias approached with caution and said, "Are you all right Pepé?"

As he extended his arms to try and catch him, Pepé feigned attack a couple of times before he calmed down enough to be caught.

Blackie peeked out from under his arms and said, "Is it safe Zach?"

Zacharias said, "Oh, yeah. It's safe, he's okay now."

Julie half whimpering said, "Are you sure Zachary?"

Zacharias said, "Yeah I'm sure Julie, hey, are you hurt? Did Pepé hurt you?"

39

Julie said, "No, no, I'm okay, it just happened so fast, it just freaked me out for a minute that's all."

Zacharias said, "Hey guys come over here and meet Pepé."

As they neared he said, "Blackie, Julie, this is my Gallo Pepé."

Blackie asked, "Can we pet him?"

Zacharias said, "Normally, yes. But he's still spooked, I can still feel him shaking a little so you better not right now."

"Oh, okay," said Blackie.

Zacharias said, "Something sure had him spooked when we came in here. I've never seen him act like that before. I wonder what it could have been?"

Julie was staring around the room and then suddenly she said, "Did you guys smell tobacco when we first came in here? I can't smell it anymore, but I could have sworn I smelled it when we ran in here."

Zacharias said, "Yeah, I smelled it."

Blackie said, "Yeah, me too, and there was something else I smelled that I half recognized, but I can't quite put my finger on it, the rush of wind dissipated it too quickly."

Julie froze, she could feel the goose flesh start at her spine and radiate out into her arms and legs, she said, "Zachary, did you feel the wind, too?"

Zacharias, sensing her fear, tried to minimize it by saying "Well, it was more like a breeze, but I'm not even sure I felt that."

"YES YOU ARE!" she said, realizing she had just been yelling, she bent her head down and stared at the floor.

Zacharias said, "Okay, yes, I did feel the wind or something rush passed us, but like how crazy is that? I mean, look around, there's not even any windows or doors in this room, we must have created a draft when we ran in."

Julie said, "NO WAY. We had already come to a complete stop before I felt something rush into us, then it was gone…and…and I don't know what the heck it was, but…."

Blackie put his arm around Julie's shoulder and said, "Hold on, hold on, we're getting ahead of ourselves. Let's not jump to conclusions, I mean what do we really know for sure?"

Zacharias said, "What I know for sure is that something scared the heck outta Pepé, I've never seen him act like that before."

Blackie said, "Well whatever it was, it's gone now, so let's get Pepé his food and water so he can eat, then we'll go have a look around."

CHAPTER 6

When Pepé was done eating, he began hopping around spreading his wings.

Blackie said, "What's he doing, Zach?"

Zacharias said, "He always does that after eating. My mami says it's a reaction to an old Mexican saying, '**pansa llena, corazon contento**' (*full stomach, happy heart*). All I know is that that's what he always does."

Zacharias shifted the flashlight beam from Pepé to the door they had come in from, then he said to Blackie and Julie, "Are you guys ready?"

Blackie said, "Okay Zach, you got point, I'll bring up the rear. We'll keep Julie between the both of us." To Julie he said, "I'm not trying to be a male-chauvinist; it's just that me and Zach each have a flashlight and you don't."

Julie said, "You won't get any argument outta me; I'm fine with being in the middle. Let's go."

As they stepped out of the room and into the hallway, to the left was the exterior door they had entered, it was still flung fully open, to the right the hallway stretched out forever, or so it seemed.

Zacharias turned right and began making his way into the dark bowels of the mansion with Blackie, Julie, and Pepé at his heels, they came to the first door on the left, Zacharias grabbed ahold of the door knob, he glanced back at them and yelled, "Are you ready?"

Before they could answer, he turned the knob and pushed leaping in and landing in a fencing stance with the flashlight in his right hand, and his right arm fully extended as if brandishing a sword, the room was completely empty, no furniture, no nothing.

Julie and Blackie were standing in the doorway with grins on their faces as Blackie says, "Hey Darth Vader, no one's here, you might wanna sheath your light-saber ole' chap!"

Julie couldn't contain her control and started giggling.

Zacharias looked back at them, and then started giggling also.

They came back out into the hallway, Blackie had his beam of light pointed straight down the corridor, at the end was what appeared to be a double-door archway.

Zacharias took the lead and said, "Stay close."

There was one more room to the right, it was also empty. As they approached the archway, the first thing that caught their sight, was the size of the colossal door knocker, they stood there admiring it for a moment, Zacharias said, "well, let's go in." he reached for the door handle and pushed, first with one arm, then with his shoulder as well, "it won't even budge," said Zacharias.

"Let's all push on it together," said Julie.

Zacharias and Blackie put their shoulders onto the door and heaved, while Julie pushed with her hands, it didn't move a millimeter; they gave up and stood back panting with exertion. Zacharias looked up at these massive doors and exclaimed, "I don't think these doors have ever been opened!"

"They have to be locked," said Julie. "We should look for a

keyhole."

Both Zacharias and Julie began running the flashlight beam all up and down the converging seam of the double doors, meticulously scrutinizing every inch.

Blackie whom had taken a couple of steps back, was staring at these double doors in a pondering almost trance like glare, suddenly he said, "Hey you two, move outta the way. I don't believe you're going to find a keyhole."

Zacharias said, "What do you mean, why not?"

Blackie said, "Well, it seems to me, that someone went to a whole lotta trouble installing that colossal door knocker, especially, on an interior door, unless....," he stepped up, grabbed ahold of the knocker, swung it up to its zenith, you could hear metal shift within, then pulled his hand away letting it drop.

It hit home with a resounding thud, swinging the doors inward, they were immediately overwhelmed by the smell of tobacco and something pungent, yet sweet.

Pepé, who had been trailing behind the three, began crowing and frantically flapping his wings, catching flight; he was thirty feet down the corridor before he came to a stop.

Zacharias chased after him. It took another minute or two before he allowed himself to be picked up and cradled by Zacharias.

Blackie said, "What the heck was that about Zach?"

Zacharias said, "I don't know, he's been acting awfully odd all morning, but I think he's okay now, come on lets go check out that room."

As they approached, the first thing they noticed was that there was a source of illumination coming from within. As they passed through the archway, Zacharias could feel Pepé shift and tense his body under his firm grasp, but the **Gallo** stayed calm not uttering a sound.

The entire right side of this vast chamber, starting about twelve feet off the ground, then slanting up at a forty five-degree angle, the whole of the roof was solar paneling, you could feel the increase in temperature instantly. The left wall was covered from floor to ceiling in books, the back wall with maps and charts, and there were several tables stacked with these items as well, immediately to the left was a rather large alcove, Blackie peered inside and said, "That's what that smell was, pecans!"

There were several gunny sacks stuffed full, some had burst at the seams and pecan nuts were scattered all over the floor. Zacharias said, "I remember my papi saying that my **Bis-Abuelo** (*great grandfather*), used to carry his pockets full of pecans, that he loved eating them."

Julie said, "This must be his private room or den."

Blackie looked at both of them and exclaimed, "You mean his SACRED CHAMBER!"

All three felt the hair on the backs of their necks instantly bristle.

Zacharias was the first one to break the silence, "Blackie, are you saying what I think your saying?"

Blackie said, "I've been bouncing it around in my head all morning; it's the only logical explanation. If there is a presence, or spirit, it has to be your **obwaylo**. No one else has ever lived here, that we know of."

Julie said, "But that doesn't make sense. I mean, why would Zachary's **obwaylo** want to scare him or chase him away?"

Blackie said, "Maybe he doesn't. Maybe he's trying to warn him or simply tell him something; we shouldn't assume that his intentions are mal-intended."

Zacharias said, "**Porque yo**? (W*hy me?*) what could he possibly want to tell me or warn me about? I agree with Julie, it doesn't make sense."

Blackie said, "What we do know is he chose you, for what or why is what we have to find out; let's start looking around and see if we can find any clues."

Julie said, "What exactly are we supposed to be looking for?"

Blackie said, "I don't know, just keep an eye out for anything unordinary."

Key of Destiny

Centering the right wall directly underneath the solar panels, strategically placed for maximum light, was a massive wooden writing desk.

Zacharias said, "I'll go look through his desk, see what I can find there." He released Pepé and as soon as Pepé was free of his grasp, he made a B-line for the alcove, not leaving any doubt as to his intentions.

There was an oversized fireplace along the back wall with maps and charts on either side of it, not saying a word, Julie wondered off in that direction.

Blackie couldn't conceal the smile on his face as he stared up at a plethora of books and historical documents that would be his domain. As his eyes began their descent, he felt an overwhelming presence, as if these giants of literature were standing alongside him, there was Homer, Dumas, Machiavelli, Danté; he was still in a state of euphoric reverie as his eyes came to a halt on a leather-bound book resting by itself on the bottom shelf.

He picked it up, tooled on the face of the book were the initials Z.G. He pulled up a chair and began to read.

Zacharias stood beside his Abuelos **escritorio** (*writing desk*) admiring the fine contours and workmanship of this maple behemoth, even the chair was finely tooled. Making his way behind the escritorio, he slowly and reverently pulled the chair back and sat in it, instantly a sense of calm washed over him, it was if he belonged to this moment, then all sound and movement seized, or so it appeared, in his mind's eye, he saw a Spanish style farmhouse complete with windmill, barn, corrals, and two beautiful palomino horses, behind all of this was a pecan orchard.

Then suddenly without warning, chaos ensued; there was an ear-splitting blast, followed by gunfire, the horror stricken screams of battle, and the unmistakable stench of cordite permeating the air.

Then, as if someone hit a light switch, everything went pitch black. Sound stopped. He felt his head start to throb. For a brief moment, he thought he may have been wounded, but quickly realized the throbbing in his head was being caused by him having had his eyes shut so tightly. He also became aware that he was squeezing the armrests with such force that his forearm muscles were beginning to spasm.

He was about to open his eyes when he felt a weight on his shoulders, as if someone's hands were resting on them, he froze, then he heard what sounded like his papi's voice say, "**Hijo, no tengas miedo** (*son, do not be afraid*).

Siempré comportaté con honor y respeto, siempré manten tu cabeza en alto, y cuando sientas que tú valor se te va, siempré recuerda que vienes de una linea de Guerreros, no solamenté la sangré mia, pero tambien la sangré de Cuahtemoc corré por tus venas.

Tú eres el escojido, pero con esto Viené mucha responsabilidad, mallormente', El guardamiento de la Llave'Del Destino nunca dejas que caiga en manos malas."

(*Always conduct yourself with honor and respect, keep your head held high, and if you sense that your courage is slipping away, remember that you descend from a line of warriors, not just my blood, but also the blood of cuahtemoc corses through your veins. You're the chosen one, but with this comes tremendous responsibility, chiefly, the guardianship of the key of destiny, never allow it to fall into evil hands.)*

Zacharias was about to open his eyes when the grip on his shoulders tightened, and he heard the voice say.

"No hijo, si habres tus ojos, nuestra coneccion se termina para siempre', solamente' te esperaba a ti'. Yo ya me puedo ir a mi descanzo, pero el viajé tuyo apenas se va empezando, y tengo - mucho que decirté, nunca...." *(No son, if you open your eyes, our connection will dissolve forever. I've been awaiting your arrival, now I can continue to my resting place, but your journey is just beginning, and I have much to tell you, never...)*

But this was as far as he gotten, from the far corner of the room Julie let out a shriek that was followed by clatter.

Zacharias opened his eyes, as he did he felt the air around him sucked upward as if from a vacuum. The next thing he knew, he was in a full sprint towards the end of the chamber the shriek had come from.

As Zacharias rounded the very last table, he saw Blackie running towards him from the opposite end, they both came to a screeching halt in front of the fireplace, rolled up maps were scattered everywhere, and Julie was flat on her back with her arms outstretched, clutching what appeared to be a wooden box.

Zacharias said, "Julie, are you hurt?"

Blackie said, "What happened?"

Julie said, "I'm okay, but I could use a little help over here!"

Both Zacharias and Blackie simultaneously said, "Oh, yeah," as they both reached down to help her up.

Blackie said, "So what happened? And what is that in your hands?"

Julie said, "This is what I was trying to reach. I put a chair atop the stepping stone of the fireplace, so that I could reach up to the mantle. I managed to get my hands on this thing, and the next thing I know, I'm bouncing off my bumm staring up at the ceiling!"

She looked straight at Zachary and said, "Hey, where did you find that key?"

Zacharias said, "What key?"

"That key," she said pointing at his chest.

Zacharias looked down at his chest area and froze, there was a skeleton key dangling there.

It was attached to a strip of leather that encircled his neck; he felt his heart skip a beat, and the goose flesh rise over his entire body.

Blackie said, "Zach, are you all right? You look as though you've seen a ghost."

Zacharias took a moment to answer, when he did, he said, "at first I thought I had been daydreaming, but Blackie I believe your right, I think I've seen a ghost!"

Then he proceeded to tell them everything he had experienced.

When he was done, Julie asked, "Do you really think it was the spirit of your **obwaylo** that spoke to you?"

Without skipping a beat Zacharias said, "I don't think, I know it was, just like I know his spirit is gone and will never return." Zacharias lifted his head and looked at both of them and said, "If it hadn't been for our intervention, he would have still been trapped here. I feel happy for him knowing that he's finally able to rest, but I'm also more confused than ever, he didn't have a chance to finish telling me everything, and we don't have a clue as to what this stupid skeleton key is for?"

Blackie said, "That may not be necessarily true."

Julie said, "What do you know that you're not telling us Blackwood, come on spill it!" When she said this, the wooden box she had been holding almost slipped outta her grasp, she flipped it over to get a better grip.

Blackie said, "Well, while Zach was having his vision, I was also contributing something productive, unlike some people, unless you think buffing the floor with your tush is going to help us somehow!" he instinctively took a step away from Julie as he said this, but it was unnecessary, for her attention was drawn by something else, she appeared to be reading something on the wooden box.

Blackie relaxed his guard and turned to Zach and was about to continue, when Julie reached over and scuffed him on the back of his head with her hand.

Blackie yelped and yelled out, "NO HITTING; WE HAVE A RULE. NO HITTING!"

Julie said, "Don't think I didn't hear what you said Blackwood!"

Blackie whimpered, "But we have a rule!"

Julie said, "Yeah, whatever."

Zacharias was giggling at these two, when suddenly they heard a noise, simultaneously all three turned and seen Pepé coming around the table, he was walking more like a penguin then a Gallo, because his belly was almost dragging on the floor. Zacharias said, "**Pepé, no te hubiera dejado solo, mira como vienes, nunca sabes cuando parar, que voy hacer contigo!**" (*"Pepé, I should have never left you alone, look at you now, you never know when to stop, what am I going* *to do with you!"*)

To this Pepé only gave a meager attempt at a crow.

Zacharias slowly shook his head from side to side in disapproval, then turned around and said, "Now what were you saying about the key Blackie?"

Blackie said, "Well, it's this book I found, look, it has the initials Z.G. tooled on the front, only it's not really a book, it's more like a day-planner, or diary, anyway, I only had time to skim over a couple of the entries, the first one I read was dated, **Abril, mil novecientos ocho, Monterey, Nuevo Leon, Mexico**, I believe that translates to (*April, 1908, Monterey, Nuevo Leon, Mexico*) Anyway, it was a story about your **obwaylo** and Pancho Villa, and their attack on a Spanish Hacienda."

Julie interrupted saying, "What's a Hacienda?"

Zacharias intervened and said, "Back in the early Sixteenth Century, when the Spanish **Conquistadores** (*conquerors*) began to colonize Mexico, each Spaniard was given a parcel of land doled out by the King of Spain. It was roughly equal to the size of a county today, unfortunately, all Mexican people living on that parcel of land, from that day forth, belonged to him, although they were paid, their salaries were nothing more than a pittance. In reality, they were nothing more than slaves! The large estates built for the Spaniards by

58

the blood and sweat of the Mexicans on these parcels of land, were called Haciendas."

Julie said, "You seem to know an awful lot about Mexican history."

Zacharias said, "I should, it's only been drilled into me by both my parents ever since I can remember, hey what else does it say Blackie?"

Blackie said, "Well, evidently, this hacienda was some sort of Central Depository, for all of the gold being extracted out of the mountains of Mexico.

It was held here until one of the Kings Spanish Galleons was made ready for its transport to Spain, anyway, your **ovwaylos** plan of attack was a success, because he and Pancho Villa made off with a wagon full of gold, it goes on to say that they split the booty equally, then it just ends, so I kept skimming pages, then a couple entries later, dated, **Julio, Mil Novecientos Ocho, Cuidad Juarez, Mexico.**"(*July 1908, Cuidad Juarez, Mexico.*)

Here he turned the book towards them and said, "This is where it gets interesting, look at this foot note here, it says, **Dondé escondo el oro!** If my Spanish hasn't failed me, I believe that means 'where do I hide the gold'*!*"

"That's exactly what it means!" said Zacharias.

Blackie continued, "It goes on to say, this I will hold interim, to give financial stability, to the next keeper of the key of destiny, then again here it simply ends, and nothing more is ever mentioned about the gold."

Julie looked at Zachary and said, "You're the next keeper of the key, so that means the gold is meant for you."

Zacharias said, "Even if the gold was still hidden, we don't have a clue as to where to look for it, I mean, it could be in Monterey. It could be in Juarez, or any other number of places in Texas."

Blackie looked straight at Zach and said, "Or here!"

Zacharias said, "You really think so?"

Blackie said, "I don't know, but I think it's just as plausible as those other places you mentioned."

Julie said, "Maybe this can help us figure it out? When I first saw it up on the mantle, what caught my eye, was the glass facing, it looks like a lava lamp, then I thought, that can't be right, they didn't make those back then, or did they?" Here she looks straight at Blackie and says, "Even though some people seem to think, that I've just been twiddling my thumbs, I'll have you know, that I took it upon myself, to risk life and limb, to retrieve what could be a very important clue!"

Zacharias said, "Well, what is it?"

Julie stammered a little and said, "Well, I'm not sure, but I have a feeling its important, first of all, look at the front. She turns the contraption towards them, "See, it has these calendar cylinders for dates or something, or maybe it's some kinda puzzle, to tell you where the gold is."

Blackie said, "I have to admit, whomever made this thing was extremely talented, it's absolutely beautiful, and it does appear that these cylinders were designed to symbolize dates, what's even more intriguing, are these cylinders on the right hand side, **pais**, means Country, and **pueblo**, means town or province, and look, count the cylinders, there's twenty nine, which corresponds with the exact number of letters in the Mexican alphabet, it's fascinating, but Julie, I still don't see any connection with this and the gold."

Julie said, "That's because you haven't seen what's on the back."

All three had ahold of it, when they flipped it over, written on the back, in the most beautiful hand writing Zacharias had ever seen, were the words, **Solamenté el encargado de la llavé, me podra manipular** (*Only the keeper of the key, can manipulate me.*)

Zacharias said, "What the heck is this thing?

Without waiting for anyone to answer, he flipped it over again so that they were looking at the front, he sat it down on the table and said, "I think Julie's right, this could be kinda like a map to tell us where the gold is. Look here where it says pais and pueblo. Let's spell out Denver, Colorado, U.S.A."

As soon as he had finished putting the A in U.S.A. there was a loud disturbance to their left, they all three jumped back a step. Julie instinctively clutched both her hands around Zachary's right arm, and Blackie had clasped his right hand onto Zach's left shoulder, but it had only been Pepé flapping his wings, he had taken flight and landed on the table.

Zacharias jutted out his chin and said, "I wasn't scared."

Both Blackie and Julie simultaneously piped in, "Me neither!"

Zacharias looked down at his arms and said, "Hey you two can let go of me now."

They both looked at him for a second, then all three started giggling. After a moment when they had regained their composure, Blackie said, "I can't make sense of this thing, even if we miraculously were to divine a location, what would be the purpose of these calendar cylinders? You would think it has to correspond to a major event back then."

Zacharias said, "The Mexican Revolution lasted from 1910 to 1920, and I'm sure there were several important battles, but the only one I know the date of by heart is, the battle over the city of Juarez,

Mexico."

He started adjusting the cylinders, when he was done it read, November Sixteenth, 1913, Juarez Mexico.

"This is the day Pancho Villa seized the city, and the point where the tide turned in favor of the Revolutionaries, but that's not why I remember the date. You could hear the sadness in his voice, as he said, "It was also the day my Abuelo died in battle."

All three were silent for a moment, and Julie had bowed her head; this was an automatic response to her Irish Catholic up-bringing. While she was in this position, something at the bottom center of the wooden box caught her eye, she leaned in closer and exclaimed, "Hey, there's a keyhole in this thing."

Both Zacharias and Blackie knelt down scrutinizing the bottom of the box, staring back at them was as old fashioned skeleton keyhole, they turned and stared at each other.

Blackie broke the silence and said, "What the heck, see if it fits."

Zacharias removed the key from around his neck and placed it in his right hand, It wasn't until he neared the keyhole that he realized his hand was shaking, he took his left hand and placed it around his right wrist to stabilize it, then inserted the key, turned it clockwise one hundred and eighty degrees he felt a surge of electricity jolt his entire body, there was what appeared to be a bolt of lightning, it was so loud and bright, it seemed to rip the very fabric of time.

It reminded Zacharias of the time his papi' had taken him to Kelly Air Force Base back in San Antonio to see the Blue Angels Perform Aerial Maneuvers. At the beginning of the show, Five F-16 Fighter Planes had flown over the crowd with such speed; it had shaken the very earth they had been standing on.

Zacharias had been staring up at these magnificent machines, when he heard a sound so loud, that it made him instinctively cup his hands over his ears, he remembered feeling scared because it had seemed as if the heavens had been split in two. His papi had put his arm around him saying, 'Don't be frightened, that's just the sound the planes make when they break the sound barrier.'

Zacharias didn't know anything about no sound barrier, all he knew, was that it had scared the heck outta him.

Julie had grabbed his arm with both of hers bringing him outta his reverie, she was screaming something at him, but he couldn't hear a thing, it was as if sound didn't exist. She was pointing at the table, he turned in that direction, it was at this very instance, that the entire scene penetrated his consciousness; the sacred chamber had become a VORTEX!!! Tables, chairs, books, everything in the room was being sucked up and outward, into what seemed an infinite abyss!

Zacharias and Julie began skidding forward, being pulled by the increasing force of this cyclonic beast.

Julie let go of Zachary with her right arm, so that she was able to reach back and catch ahold of the wooden railing that was about four feet in front of the table.

When Zacharias turned around, he saw Blackie take two steps towards them; then his vision seemed to shift beyond them. Blackie froze as if in a moment of indecision, then in what Zacharias took as a deliberate act of INSANITY!

He witnessed Blackie run and leap past them towards the very JAWS OF THE BEAST! Zacharias couldn't believe what he was seeing! THIS WAS THE STUFF OF NIGHTMARES!

Zacharias jerked his head around in time to see Pepé being sucked across the table, leaving claw marks in his wake, and Blackie land on the table to one side of him.

He snatched Pepé up in his arms, pulling him into his chest, and rolling onto his stomach, pinning him there.

Blackie had curled his toes over the edge of the table; this was the only thing holding him from being sucked out into the abyss.

Zacharias stretched-out his left hand but couldn't quite reach him.

Julie saw Zachary's head turn towards her and he seemed to be yelling something at her, but no sound escaped his lips.

She couldn't understand any of this!

Zacharias pulled his leg up and motioned for her to release his arm, and grab him by the bottom of his pant leg. Having done this, he was able to stretch-out and secured a firm grip on one of Blackie's tennis shoes. But in doing so, he dislodged the toe grip that had been anchoring Blackie down.

Blackie and Pepé were now levitated in mid-air, their bodies being tossed around like rag dolls.

Zacharias felt Blackie's foot begin to slip out of his shoe; he squeezed the tennis shoe with every last ounce of strength he could muster. He felt a JOLT, and knew before he even looked up, THAT BLACKIE AND PEPÉ WERE GONE!

Zacharias felt as if someone had reached into his gut and yanked out a rib, then what was even worse, he heard the sound of his Papi's voice in his head saying, '**Un hombre tiene que ser responsable por las decisiones que hace, especialmente' cuando afecta el bien estar de otros.**' (A *man has to be responsible for the decisions he makes, especially when they concern the well being of others.*)

It struck him like a rock, that ultimately, it was his decision to involve Blackie, Julie, and Pepé, they were his responsibility, and he had failed!

Zacharias was twisting his body around to face Julie when something struck him in the chest, it was the wooden box, he was about to fling it aside, when in that second, something flashed within him; he couldn't have said what it was, but something deep within him, impelled him, and he knew in that moment, that he mustn't part with it.

When he looked back at Julie, there were tears streaming down her cheeks, and the blank look of shock on her face.

His heart caught in his throat, he knew what he had to do, but didn't think he had the heart to pry himself away and leave her alone.

Julie had been watching him the entire time; she had witnessed the array of emotions flashing across his face, SORROW, FAILURE, SHAME, then she saw the familiar jutting of the jaw, and the resolve in his demeanor, all of this was a reminder to her, of his never wavering moral compass, in short, everything she had come to admire in him.

Zacharias placed his free foot against her wrist that was holding his pant leg, and began trying to pry away.

Julie jerked on his leg, knocking his prying foot away.

Zacharias looked straight into her eyes, and to his surprise, saw the look of shock vanish, she almost looked happy, then she mouthed the words "ALL FOR ONE, AND ONE FOR ALL!"

She was still smiling, as she purposely allowed her hand to release the railing.

CHAPTER 8

Zacharias and Julie were tumbling into what felt like outer space, gravity was non-existent, Julie had wrapped both her arms around Zachary's leg, then they saw what looked like small electrical surges igniting all around them, all of this culminated into a burst of light, they both instinctively shut their eyes, then in the next second they felt an impact, they rolled twice and came to a stop.

When Zacharias opened his eyes, he found himself staring up at a cloudy sky, complete with the last vestiges of stars one see's before the dawning of a new day.

He was beginning to think that it had all been a dream, when he felt Julie tug on his leg and say, "Zachary, are we alive?" Zacharias sat bolt-upright clutching the wooden box to his chest. He said, "Julie, are you okay?

Are you hurt?"

He sat the wooden box aside and began to help her up.

Julie said, "Zachary, where are we?" Then she turned and looked at the wooden box and asked, "And what the heck is that thing?"

Zacharias said, "I'm not shhhh…"

But before he could finish, Julie interrupted him saying, "LOOK AROUND! WE'RE OUTSIDE FOR HEAVEN'S SAKE! AND WHERE'S THE FREAKING MANSION?"

Zacharias looked to the east where the sun had just begun cresting over the horizon, it wasn't fully light yet, but from what he could see, they appeared to be on some kind of footpath or trail that skirted a grouping of foothills.

He was still trying to figure out what had happened, and where they were, for that matter, when Julie began tugging on his shirt - sleeve. When he turned to her, she was pointing her finger up the trail, as he turned in that direction following her line-of-sight, he saw two Mexican boys about their own age coming towards them.

They were about fifteen yards away; the one in the lead was wearing some three quarter-length trousers and nothing more, no shirt, no shoes, nothing.

He carried a staff, or some kind of stick with him, and his face was streaked in what looked like black paint.

The one behind was almost entirely naked, except for what appeared to be some kind of loin-cloth, and he also had no shoes, he was holding onto a rope that was draped over his shoulder, there was something attached to it dangling down his back, but Zacharias couldn't see what it was.

The one in the lead took two more steps and froze, as he glanced up the trail and caught sight of them, immediately he gripped his staff with both hands, and positioned his legs in a defensive stance, you could see the muscles in his chest and arms tighten and ripple in anticipation.

The one that had been bringing up the rear, let loose of the rope that had been straddling his shoulder, whatever he had been carrying, dropped to the ground like a stone, without skipping a beat, he bent down and picked up a dirt-clod the size of a grapefruit, he came forward and took a stance alongside his companion.

The one carrying the staff, peeled his lips away from his teeth, and exclaimed, "**GRINGOS**" (*white people*) as they both took two more steps towards them narrowing the gap.

Zacharias sensed the imminent presence of danger, the transformation that had taken place within these two had been almost animalistic. Zacharias said, "**yo no soy gringo, soy tejano**." ("*I'm not a white person, I'm Texan.*)

The one with the staff said, "**Entonces lo que tenemos aqui, es una gringa, y un traidor!**" (*Then what we have here, is a white girl, and a traitor!*).

Zacharias having heard this Mexican boy utter these last words with such disdain, (*became fully aware of his mistake*) although he hadn't fully committed to the scenario that his brain was telling him was fact, he knew enough about Mexican history, to be aware of the views held by Mexicans towards Texans, (R*emember the Alamo*) kept running through his head, this Anglo battle cry was symbolic to Mexicans, they couldn't forgive the Mexicans living in what is today, TEXAS, for throwing in with the gringos and fighting against Mexico, to establish Texas as its own republic (*hither-to, branded by Mexicans as traitors.*).

The Mexican boy whom up until this point hadn't uttered a word, said, "**He escuchado los hombres en la plaza decir que los gringos americanos se rescatan por mucho dinero, vamos a llevarnos a la gringa.**" (*I've overheard the men in the town square say, that you can* *ransom white Americans for lots of money, let's take the white girl.*)

As the boys began to advance towards them, Zacharias could hear his Abuelos words in his head, **La sangré mia, y la Sangre de Cuahtemoc, corré por tus venas.**" (*mine and cuahtemoc's blood, courses through your veins.*)

Before he knew what he was doing, he had stepped over in front of Julie and said, "**No, ella es mi amiga**." (*No! She's my friend.*)

The Mexican boy was so quick, Zacharias didn't have time to react, the impact struck him on the left side of his head, it was a glancing blow, but still hard enough to stun him, then he caught sight of the other Mexican boy advancing with his staff held high ready to strike.

Zacharias' left ear was still ringing, when he thought he heard a familiar battle cry somewhere behind him, before his brain could make any sense of this, he saw a streak of red pass inches away from the right side of his head.

The next thing he knew, Pepé had his talons embedded in the forehead and scalp of the Mexican boy with the staff, the boy immediately dropped his weapon and began trying to tug Pepé off his head.

Even though Pepé was a great grandpa himself, he still had the strength of a Gallo half his age, and he wasn't about to surrender the purchase he had on this boys scalp.

Seeing this, Zacharias let loose his own battle cry, screaming, "CUAHTEEEMMOOOOC!" As he ran head first into the midsection of the boy Pepé had ahold of, they all three hit the ground, as Zacharias turned his head to the left, he realized he had made a terrible mistake, the other boy had picked up the staff, and was poised ready to strike.

Zacharias still had his arms around the mid-section of the Mexican boy on the ground, there wasn't any time, all he could do was shut his eyes, tuck his head, and try an absorb the blow, his body tensed in anticipation, he heard the impact, and what sounded like the crack of bone, but the adrenaline was pumping through his body so fast, he didn't feel a thing, he opened his eyes and turned his head to the left, the Mexican boy was raising the staff a second time, when he was at his fullest extension, ready to bring down his swing, Zacharias saw someone slam into the Mexican boy with such force, they both left the ground landing about six feet away.

The Mexican boy Zacharias had ahold of was struggling to get away, Zacharias looked up and saw rivulets of blood flowing down the boys face, he got scared and let him go.

The Mexican boy bounced to his feet and began running wildly down the trail from where they had come.

Zacharias by now had come to the conclusion, that it must have been Blackie, whom had come to his rescue.

He jumped to his feet and ran over to help him; when he got to them, Blackie was straddling the boy, pummeling him with reckless abandon.

Zacharias screamed, "BLACKIE STOP!" as he reached down and began to pry him off the boy, he tugged so hard they both fell over backwards.

By the time they both got to their feet, the Mexican boy had one arm wrapped around his ribs and was half jogging half running down the trail.

Blackie looked at Zach, as if seeing him for the first time and said, "Hey ole' chap, you seem no worse for wear, old Pepie and I were coming around that bluff, just in time as it turns out, but I gotta hand it to Pepie, he sensed the danger before I did, he shot passed me like a bullet, the next thing I know, I saw that Mexican boy blindside you with that rock, I must say, I thought you was done for."

Zacharias said, "It wasn't a rock, it was a dirt-clod, and he half missed me with it, but I'll tell you what, I'm starting to feel it now."

Blackie said, "Hey where's Julie?"

They both turned and saw her kneeling down with her head bowed, as they approached, Zacharias was thinking, what's she doing?

Then he caught sight of a pile of red feathers directly in front of her.

He screamed, "Pepé!" as he ran and dropped to his knees next to Julie; he took one look at Pepé and knew he was no-more.

He had been around Gallo's all of his life, and had witnessed death claim the lives of many brave warriors, yet his brain couldn't accept it, he felt Julie's hand slip into his and squeeze, he looked over at her, she still had her head bowed, and there were tears streaming down her cheeks, but she refused to make eye contact, everything hit him like a ton of bricks, and worst of all, he couldn't get his papi's words outta his head. **"Un hombre no llora delante de una mujer."** (A *man never cries in front of a woman.*)

He felt a sting in his eyes, and knew he was going to let his papi' down. He pulled his hand free from Julie's, jumped to his feet and ran as fast as he could out into the open field towards the rising sun.

He didn't stop until he knew he was far enough away not to be heard, then he allowed himself to drop to the ground and begin to sob, his first thoughts were, what a fool he had been, in the arrogance he had displayed, in believing he had absorbed the first blow of the staff, and not felt it. (He cursed himself out loud, of course he hadn't felt it;

it wasn't he that was struck!)

What a fool he was for thinking he could conduct himself as a man, he had failed Pepé, and was now crying in front of a girl all in the same day, what a pathetic excuse for a boy, much less a man!

Then he felt his papi's eyes upon him, and began feeling ashamed for having felt sorry for himself, and if Pepé could see him now, what would he think? He looked up at the heavens, and swore an oath to Pepé, he vowed to see this thing through or die trying.

When he turned to go back and join his friends, he felt more alive and with purpose, then he had ever felt before. He had also promised Pepé to never take his life for granted, and to be accountable to his family and friends, and to conduct himself in a manner that would never illicit shame.

As Zacharias approached Blackie and Julie, he noticed they were standing over a mound of dirt.

Blackie turned towards him and said, "I couldn't see any reason to leave him lying out, I hope you don't mind?"

Zacharias replied, "Oh, no, not at all, as a matter of fact, I would like to thank, you and Julie both, for doing this for Pepé."

Zacharias noticed they had even erected a makeshift crucifix at the head of the grave.

Julie said, "Zachary would you like to say a few words?"

Zacharias looked at both of them for a moment, then said, "At first I felt sad, hurt, and even abandoned I guess, until I realized, I should feel proud of Pepé, proud, because he was one of the bravest **Gallo Guerrero** (*rooster warriors*) that ever lived, and loyal to the end, for he truly died a hero's death, engaging the enemy on the field of battle—nothing is greater to a warrior than this privilage, **Murio como Vivio, con honor y dignidad**. (*He died as he lived, with honor and dignity.*)

Whenever my time comes, I can only hope to display the courage that Pepé did. Then he turned to the heavens and said, "**Nunca te olvidaré mi amigo**! (*I will never forget you my friend!*)

CHAPTER 9

All three were standing over Pepé's grave when Blackie said, "I hate to put an end to this, but we need to talk, and we need to talk now!"

He reached down and picked up the wooden box that Julie had placed near Pepé's grave; staring back at him was November sixteenth, 1913, Juarez, Mexico.

He noticed the strap of leather dangling from the bottom, he grabbed ahold of the key and turned it counter clockwise one hundred and eighty degrees.

Both Julie and Zacharias exclaimed, "WHAT ARE YOU DOING!"

Blackie ignored them and pulled on the key, it slid right out. He looked at Zach and said, "I believe this belongs to you."

Zacharias grabbed it and began placing it around his neck, while Blackie continued, "I'm not sure how much of this you've already figured out, or if your even willing to believe or accept.

But here's what I do know, over the years, some of the greatest minds ever produced, have subscribed to the theory of parallel universes, windows in time so to speak, and have even proven, in theory, that such quantum leaps are possible.

I myself have been open-minded, although I harbored certain reservations.

This morning when Pepie and I came through that porthole, we landed atop that ridge over yonder, from up there, you can see a town to the west, it's a couple of miles away, but I can assure you, that there's a heck of a lot of activity over there.

At first sight, I thought I was witnessing a lightning and thunder storm, then I saw it for what it really was—THERE'S A BATTLE BEING WAGED IN THAT TOWN!

Blackie took a moment then continued. "I was staring at this scene in utter disbelief; how could this be? I remember questioning my sanity, and thinking I had lost all sense of reality, it was at this point that I realized something was wrong, something about this whole scene wasn't making sense, then I remembered the wooden box, and the key of destiny.

Then it hit me like a ton of bricks, *it was what I wasn't seeing*, that was wrong. There weren't any skyscrapers, neon lights, nor automobiles that I could see, not to mention the lack of an aerial attack, where were the F-16, there was no activity in the air what-so-ever. If you add all that up, and throw two Mexican boys into the mix, one can only infer, that we've landed, RIGHT SMACK IN THE MIDDLE OF THE MEXICAN REVOLUTION!!!

Julie had been staring straight at Blackie intently listening to everything he had said, when he had finished, she turned away as if not fully comprehending, when her line of sight came to rest on a chunk of mass plopped in the center of the trail, she took two steps towards it and exclaimed,

"WHAT IN TARNATIONS IS THAT?"

Zacharias and Blackie both turned and assumed a defensive stance, before focusing in on what she had seen.

Zacharias said, "That's an armadillo."

As they closed in on it Blackie said, "It's a dead armadillo, look its feet are bound with that length of rope."

Zacharias said, "That must have been what that Mexican boy had strapped over his shoulder."

Julie said, "An arma-what?"

Zacharias said, "Haven't you ever seen an armadillo before?"

Julie said, "Heck no! When I first saw it, I thought it was something prehistoric, you know, like a tiny brontosaurus or something."

Blackie said, "Excellent!"

Julie said, "What's excellent?"

Blackie said, "The armadillo. Don't you see, that obviously fortifies my theory."

Julie said, "YOUR THEORY, WHAT THE HECK ARE YOU TALKING ABOUT BLACKWOOD? COME ON SPILL IT!"

Blackie gave Julie a menacing sideways glance as he said, "As almost the entire civilized world knows, armadillos inhabit South and Central America, and the Southern-most part of North America. The climate in Denver is not conducive for their habitation, and that's why

Julie's never seen one, because it's simply too cold there. (Here he turned to face Julie and said) And what does that mean?"

But, before she could utter a sound, he continued, "IT MEANS WE'RE NOT IN KANSAS ANYMORE DOROTHY!!!"

Zacharias started giggling but quickly stopped, when he saw Julie doubling up her fists and squaring off to Blackie. But Blackie, anticipating this, had quickly taken two steps back. Zacharias jumped in-between them and said, "Come on, knock it off you two, this is serious!" but he was still giggling inside. Suddenly he turned somber and said, "I've been thinking about this, and I keep coming back to the key of destiny. My Abuelo entrusted it to me, that tells me, I'm meant to be here, it's my destiny, but after what happened to Pepé, well, it made me realize that this isn't a game, and I have no right to endanger you two."

"Now hold on just a minute," interrupted Julie. "I, for one, *chose* to be part of this journey, danger or no danger; we're in this together, look around you Zachary, it's not just you, we're all three here together, that tells me, our destinies are intertwined, we're also meant to be here, why?, I don't know, maybe it's to help you find the gold, or maybe it's because we need each other to make it back, or fate has something in store for us, whatever the reason, we stick together, and I won't have any more talk about it!"

Blackie turned to Zach and said, "She's right ole' chap, whether we chose it, or it chose us, makes no difference."

"YOUR DARN TOOTIN' IT DOESN'T," said Julie.

Blackie said, "So then that's settled."

Zacharias knew that he should consider this more carefully, but knowing that he had already been defeated, heard himself say, "All right, but from here on out we stick together."

Julie said, "Zachary, before we go on, there's something else I need to know.

I heard you mention him before, and again when you spearheaded that Mexican boy, you yelled-out Quartz-Amok or something, who was he?"

Zacharias said, "Oh, you mean, Cuahtemoc!"

Julie said, "Yeah that guy; didn't your great grandpa say that he was related to you?"

Zacharias said, "It's still hard for me to believe, I mean I've learned about Cuahtemoc all of my life, and now to know that I'm related to him, it's unreal, and awesome all at the same time, anyway, the story goes that back in 1519, Hernan Cortez and his Conquistadores entered the city of Tenochtitlan, modern day Mexico

City, under the guise of friendship, then they took the Aztec ruler Moctezuma II hostage, and barricaded themselves in a palace, the Aztec warriors began preparations for an attack, but were urged by Moctezuma II, because he was in fear for his life, to cooperate, even though they wanted to attack, they had to respect their rulers decision.

A few months later and desperate for revenge, the Aztecs attacked the Spaniards and their allies. These were the tribes in the region that were at odds with the Aztecs, whom the Spaniards had Coerced and Bribed, in order to align themselves with them. Moctezuma II was persuaded by the Spaniards, to climb up on the palace roof and call for peace; again, the Aztec warriors obeyed, but lost all faith in their ruler. This situation continued for several months, keep in mind, that the Spaniards brought the Bubonic Plague, and Small Pox Virus, to the continent with them when they invaded. This decimated the Tenochtitlan population; it had been thriving with over a quarter of a million people, and now had literally been wiped-out by the Black Death. Approximately sixty thousand people survived, a tenth of these being warriors, all were severally weakened, not only from the virus, but also from lack of nutrition, due to the siege of the city. Moctezuma II died, some say by the hands of his own people, other accounts say he was strangled by the Spaniards, for he no longer served any purpose, either way, the Aztec people elected Cuahtemoc their new ruler. He vowed to protect his city and his people to the death, all supported him, not only warriors, but women and children joined in battle in defense of their beloved city.

In the melee that ensued, Cuahtemoc was wounded, captured, and taken prisoner; the Spaniards tortured him in many ways, even burning his feet over an open fire, and still he would not give the word for his people to surrender.

In the end, they killed him, and eventually won the war over the city of Tenochtitlan, but to this day, Cuahtemoc is remembered in history as being the bravest and most loyal of Aztec rulers." Julie said, "WOW, YOU'RE RELATED TO A REAL HERO!"

Blackie said, "Zach, you share the blood of kings and warriors." He placed his hand on Zach's shoulder and asked, "Do you still doubt that we can finish what we started?"

Zacharias having been caught up in the moment and feeling a new sense of confidence, jutted out his chin and said, "Blackie, give me a hand untying the rope from the armadillo. We'll use it to build a make-shift sling, so that we can strap the wooden box to our backs."

To Julie he said, "Go get the staff, we may need a weapon."

CHAPTER 10

As they made their preparations to depart, Blackie said, "When I was up on the ridge viewing the battle, I also noticed a rather large farm house to the south, and two smaller adobe' built dwelling in the distance. He looked straight at Zach and said, "The larger one was of distinctly different architecture, and taking into account what you told us earlier, I believe it to be a Hacienda. I don't know about you two, but I'm certainly not in a rush to go walking into a battle without knowing what's going on. I say we make for the Hacienda and see if we can find out where your obwaylo and Pancho Villa are, so we can figure out a way to get word to them."

Zacharias said, "That does sound better then walking into a war zone, but we need to hurry, you two already know why this particular day in history is so significant to me!"

Blackie felt the contraction in his bowels that a person experiences, when fear triggers the release of adrenaline through the body, he sensed danger but at the moment couldn't quite piece it together in his brain, before he could fully process the implications of Zach's last statement, Julie broke his train of thought by saying.

"Zachary, I know you said that this Pancho Villa guy was a Captain or Lieutenant in the Revolution, but like, who was he? I mean, why was he so famous?"

Zacharias said, "Come on let's get going, I'll tell you on the way."

As they began walking south along the foothills he said, "First of all, he wasn't a Captain, he was a General in the Revolution, but to really understand him, I'll have to start from the beginning. When Pancho Villa, whose real name was Doroteo Arango, was about Thirteen years old, he along with his mother and sister, whom, was a couple of years older, all worked as **Peones** (*peasants, persons held in servitude*.) for the local Hacienda.

Doroteo and his mother both worked the fields; his sister had recently been selected as a chamber-maid. On this particular day, something had happened to one of the mules out in the field, and Doroteo was bringing him back to the stables. Upon entering, Doroteo caught the **Haciendado** (*Spanish lord*) forcing himself on his sister."

Julie, whom had been listening intently, interrupted saying, "Zachary, do you mean to say that he was raping her?"

Zacharias answered, "Yes, yes. That's exactly what I mean." He continued, "The only thing Doroteo possessed (that belonged to his father) was a Colt-45 handgun, he had made it common practice (for the protection of his family) to never leave the perimeter of the Hacienda without it.

In this moment of rage, he pulled the Gun and shot the Hacendado.

He and his sister ran out into the field to alert their mother as to what had transpired, upon hearing the news, his mother gave Doroteo the few coins she had at her disposal, and urged him to run and hide himself in the mountains, she told him straight out, Doroteo, it doesn't matter the situation, you're a **Mestizo** (*halfbreed, half Spanish, half Mexican*) you have no rights under the law, and you've shot a True blood Spanish Lord, they'll hunt you down like a dog, and they will kill you—do not allow yourself to be caught!'

In the mountains were where the Highway men/Bandits, made their home. They would come down out of the mountains to rob stagecoaches and rich merchants out in the open roads. This was where Doroteo fled too, his first encounter with these bandits, didn't go well, and even though he was big for his age, and had learned early on to defend himself, he was no match for them, they disarmed him, robbed him of the few coins he had, and beat him unconscious. He awoke in the middle of the night bloodied and beaten; he passed the wee hours of the morning cold and miserable.

At first light he heard the thundering of hooves as the bandits returned, he was too weak to run, so he resolved himself to stand and face whatever blow life had in-store for him.

They encircled him, Doroteo instinctively doubled up his fists, awaiting the onslaught, but to his surprise, only one of the riders dismounted.

As he approached, Doroteo noticed he was smiling.

The man said, "**Como te llamas muchacho**?"" (*What's your name boy?*)"

He answered him, "Doroteo Arango."

The man slowly shook his head up and down as if confirming something and said, "**Yo soy el jefé de nuestros bandidos, me llamo Jorge Villa.**" "(*I'm the boss of our band of bandits, my name is George Villa.*)" The man stretched out his hand as if in friendship and said, "**Disculpenos por tratarté como un cualquiera no me llego palabra de lo que habias hecho, hasta esta mañana.**" (*Forgive us for treating you as a person of no consequence, we had no word of your deeds until this morning.*)

Doroteo reached out and shook his hand.

Jorge continued, "**Tratar de quitarlé la vida,a uno de los opresores de la genté Mexicana (por mas de trescientos años) es el acto mas respetado entre los bandidos.**" (*To attempt to take the life of one of the men whom have oppressed the Mexican people (for over three hundred years) warrants the ultimate respect of each and every bandit.*)

Jorge smirked and said, "**No te voy a devolver tú dinero, y que eso sea la primer regla que aprendas de mi, nunca devuelvas el dinero que te has robado. Pero la arma para que un hombré se defienda, es completamenté otra cosa, (aqui Jorge le da su arma para atras.) y quiero que sepas, que nuestra casa es tu casa.**" (*I'm not going to return your money, and let that be the first rule you learn from me, never return the money you have stolen, but to take away the weapon a man has to defend himself with, is another thing entirely, (here he hands Doroteo back his gun.) And I want you to know, that our home is your home.*)

Doroteo says, "**Gracias** (*thank you*) but I think the federales will be searching for me high and low, and I do not wish to bring them down on you."

Jorge says, "Entonces te tendremos que cambiar el nombre, estas medio panson muchacho, le das un Parecido a un Francisco,- o- Pancho por corto. Si, desde' este dia para adelanté, seras conocido por el nombre' PANCHO VILLA." *George says, "(then we shall change your name, you're a rather pudgy boy, you remind me of a francisco, or pancho for short. Yes!From this day forth, you shall be known by the name, Pancho villa!)"*

Zacharias took a moment to gather his thoughts, then continued, "It was society and circumstance, that made Pancho a bandit, but none the less a bandit he became, and not just a bandit, but the most notorious bandit in all of Mexico. Years passed, then in Nineteen Ten, when the Revolution was about to kick-off. The heads of the Revolutionary engine approached Pancho Villa. They asked if he would support the cause of the Mexican people, in over-throwing the dictatorship of Porfirio Diaz. In return, when the Revolution succeeded, he would be pardoned for all his previous banditry; a clean slate so to speak.

Pancho asked, "What exactly will I be doing?" They told him that they wanted him and his gang to rob federal shipments of gold, and to raid and pillage the haciendas of known sympathizers in order to fund the Revolution. They agreed to allow him to keep a percentage of all his gains, in order for him to feed and pay his army. To Pancho's way of thinking, they were just giving legitimacy for him to continue to do what he had always done. There was nothing to ponder, he was in.

Zacharias was silent a moment, then continued, "From the very beginning, because of his notoriety, he was made the poster child of the Revolution, keep in mind, that due to the dictatorship of Porfirio Diaz, the economy was such, that roughly three percent of the Mexican population, garnered all gains, and were extremely rich, while the remaining ninety seven percent of the population were dirt poor. A middle class just simply didn't exist. This is why PANCHO became symbolic of the poor man's struggle against government; this, coupled with his brave and daring successful robberies, elevated him to the status of National Hero! Here Zacharias stopped in mid-stride, turned to face them and said, in my opinion, up until this point in his life, he had been nothing more than a product of his environment; a ruthless bandit, but from here on in, because of his alignment with the Revolution, he began to hear the praises for his exploits by the Mexican people. Everywhere he went, he witnessed the admiration in his fellow **paisanos** (countrymen's) eyes. He began to buy into the idea of championing the cause, and fighting for those less fortunate.

During his years with the Revolution, he befriended Francisco Madero He was an educated mestizo and the Revolutionary heads selection for President, once the Revolution was won.

These two were known for having discussions that lasted all

through the night, even though Pancho had no formal schooling, he was very astute, he slowly began to understand the patterns of behavior, that kept the poor from pulling themselves out of poverty.

Madero told him that the real change would come from the future fathers of Mexico, 'our children will one day rule Mexico'.

This struck a chord with Pancho, for from here on out, every town he ravaged, he would gather all dictator sympathizers, and demand their money or their lives, but before leaving the town, he would call on the local Catholic Priest, and give him money with the instructions to hire a teacher to educate the young poor children of the town.

In doing so, he felt he was breaking the cycle, or patterns of behavior, that kept his people in poverty. He understood that education was the key!

Zacharias paused a moment, then said, "I want you to know that I'm not diminishing his cruelty. He was known as a strict disciplinarian with his men, those who crossed the line, usually paid with their lives. He was a leader of men, and conducted himself as such. After the Revolution, these towns that started these makeshift teaching facilities began to apply for federal assistance to build schools for public learning from the newly installed government of the people. So again, in my opinion, one could make a case for Pancho Villa, stating that he was the founder of the public school system in Mexico.

That was Pancho Villa in a nut shell. Hey you two, we better keep it down, we're getting close."

Key of Destiny

CHAPTER 11

As they approached, there was no visible activity to be seen, Zacharias began looking around, and then said, "It feels like I've been here before." Then he froze.

Julie noticed the look of bewilderment on his face and said, "What is it, what's wrong?"

Zacharias said, "I think this is the place my Abuelo showed me in my trance, or vision, or whatever the heck it was. I mean it looks the same, the windmill, the corrals, the barn."

Julie interrupted saying, "And there are some trees in the back."

"Julie, look at their conformity, those are not just random trees, that's a pecan orchard!" said Blackie.

All three looked at each other; Zacharias was the first one to speak, saying, "If this is the place, where are the palomino horses?"

"We need to go check the barn, if they're in there, then there isn't any doubt," said Blackie.

Zacharias said, "Why don't we just go knock on the door and see if..."

Blackie interrupted saying, "And see if what? What if he's not there? No one else is going to believe us; plus, there's something else we need to talk about, and I don't think you're going to like it."

"What do you mean I'm not gonna like it?" said Zacharias, instantly feeling defensive.

Blackie said, "Well, awhile back, when you said that we should hurry because of the significance of this day in history, something was tugging at my conscience, I felt a sense of dread, but I couldn't have told you at the time why. Then on the way here, it came to me."

Here he looked straight into Zach's eyes and said, "I don't know! No one knows for that matter the true effects that our actions here have on the future. They could be catastrophic! We have to be extremely careful, so no matter what, we cannot alter the course of history, I won't allow it!

Zacharias was fit to be tied, when he said in a rage, "YOU! YOU WON'T ALLOW IT! Let me tell you one thing Blackie; don't you go speaking for me! My papi always tells me, a true man always makes his own decisions, never allow another man to make your mind up for you!"

Blackie shot back, "That may be so, but look in the mirror Zach, We're not men, we're boys, and we did come here together!"

Zacharias reached up and clasped the key that had been dangling around his neck, and yanked it off. He threw it on the ground at Blackie's feet, and said, "You can go back anytime you want, but I for one am gonna finish what I started!" Then he spun around and turned his back on Blackie.

Blackie leaned over, scooped up the key and said, "Don't think I'll hesitate to leave you here!"

Julie who had been listening to these two in utter disbelief said, "You don't really mean that Blackie?"

Blackie said, "BULLOCKS IF I DON'T!" He spun on his heels and began walking towards the barn, then hesitated a moment and yelled over his shoulder, "I'LL GIVE YOU GUY'S FIVE MINUTES, THEN I'M OUTTA HERE!"

Zacharias yelled back, "Don't hold your breath!"

Julie had had enough of this, she spun around to face Zachary, and using both hands, she shoved him in the chest as hard as she could.

Zacharias flew backwards about three feet, but was able to keep his balance and remain upright, he was stunned, but before he could articulate anything, Julie let him have it, "YOUR ACTING LIKE A TOTAL JERK, ZACHARY! Blackie was right, you're always saying a man this and a man that! News flash!! You're not a man...yet! And yes, maybe Blackie was wrong, or at least arrogant in assuming he could decide something for all of us, but he has a point. We don't know what were getting into, or how it will affect the future. What if your Obwaylo was to survive and marries again; does that mean that you'll never be born? Or that you cease to exist in the future?"

Zacharias, who hadn't thought any of this through, realized, that in fact, he had been a total jerk, and was about to say so, when the thundering of hooves penetrated his consciousness. Before he could fully comprehend what was taking place, it was too late. An entire cavalry of horsemen were upon them.

Zacharias looked up and locked eyes with the lead rider (in this moment of recognition) everything that ensued was instantaneous, but to Zacharias, everything played out in slow motion. He could hear the pounding of his heart in his ears. He turned and grabbed Julie by the hand and yelled, "RUUUNNN!"

They both began running, but to Zacharias, it felt as if they were running in molasses. As if the Grim Reaper himself, was tugging at their shirt tails. He knew the lead rider was in pursuit, before he turned to look, but look he did, the realization that his worst nightmare had manifested itself, seemed to Zacharias, to have been decreed by Satan himself.

El Demonio (*the demon*) and his horse were almost atop of them, Zacharias' heart skipped a beat, when he saw the sabor El Demonio was wielding over his head. To Zacharias it seemed as if he could feel the heat on his back, that escaped the nostrils of the beast the Demonio was riding.

It was at this moment that Julie stumbled and sent them both tumbling into a maelstrom of arms, legs, and tumbleweeds. When this insanity stopped, they found themselves flat on their backs.

Zacharias was still seeing stars, when a hand reached outta the heavens and snatched him up by the scruff of the neck. He was thrown over the horse's mane like a sack of potatoes. It was at this point that Zacharias sensed more than seen a second horse and rider, he tried to shift his body, because the saddle horn was digging into his side, but was too weak to do so. The last thing he heard was Julie whimper, as she too was snatched up, then the lights went out.

Zacharias awoke as the Demonio brought his beast to a complete stop, then he heard the exchange of gunfire not too far off in the distance, then the thundering of hooves that marked the arrival of a second party.

Zacharias felt as if he had been worked-over with a baseball bat, he tried to raise his head in order to survey the situation, but was too weak to do so, then what appeared to be a golden horse, came to a stop directly in Zacharias' line of sight. Although he could only see from its belly down to its hooves, and the boots of the man riding it, he instinctively knew that the voice that ensued came from this man.

"Que es lo que tenemos aqui?"(*"What is it that we have here?"*)

Zacharias heard the Demonio respond, **"Son gringos del otro lado, mi General**." (*"Their whites from the other side, my general."*)

"Y como por dios llegaron aqui?" (*"And how in God's name did they arrive here?"*)

El Demonio said, **"No se mi General, pero damé solamenté cinco minutos con ellos, y te lo juro que cantaran como un perico."** (*"I don't know my general, but allow me a mere five minutes with them, and I swear to you, that they will sing like parakeets."*)

A second golden horse pulled alongside the Demonio, obstructing Zacharias' view of the Generals horse. Then abruptly, his head was jerked up by the hair, and he came face to face with his Bis-Abuelo! There was no doubt what-so-ever, it was as if he was looking at an older version of his papi.

For a moment, Zacharias thought he saw these familiar features, dance around the edges of recognition then quickly dissipate, as General Pancho Villas voice rang out. **"La Revolucion no espera a ninguno! Los Soldados de Porfirio Diaz ya Vienen avanzando!"** (*"The revolution waits for no one! Porfirio diaz' soldiers are advancing upon us!"*)

Here Zacharias musters the strength to tug on his Abuelo's boot, and says, **"Eres mi Bisabuelo."** (*"You're my Great-Grandfather."*) He notices his Bisabuelos eyes widen ever so slightly, then Pancho Villas' voice rings out, "Fierro!"

El Demonio answers, **"A sus ordenes mi General."** (*"At your command my general."*)

PANCHO VILLA continues, **"Encierrame' a estos dos en el sotano, hasta que acabemos con esta batalla."** (*"Lock these two up in the cellar until we put an end to this battle.'* Then in his war voice says, **"Compañia adelanté!"**(*"Company advance!"*)

Upon hearing this command, his Abuelo releases the grip he had on his hair, and begins to move away.

Zacharias knew this was his only chance, but his mouth was so encrusted with dust he was finding it hard to produce saliva. He willed himself to choke out the words, "**Abuelo, la llavé**." ("*Grandfather, the key.*") again, his view was limited to the animals belly, and legs of horse and rider.

Zacharias wasn't even sure whether his Abuelo had heard him or not, although, he thought he had seen the horse being pulled back in mid stride.

Then PANCHO VILLA'S voice rang out, "**Capitan, a mi mano derecha!**" ("C*aptain, to my right side!*") Then in the next second his Abuelo was gone.

Zacharias began to see stars, like one see's when the brain is being deprived of oxygen, off in the distance, he heard Pancho Villa's voice ring out "**VIVA LA REVOLUCION!**" ("*The revolution lives!*") Then the thundering of hooves as the cavalry departed in a hail of bullets; his last thoughts before losing consciousness were, it isn't fair, it's not supposed to end like this.

CHAPTER 12

Zacharias awoke to Julie kneeling over him like a mother hen, he said, "What happened? Where are we?" He sat up and instantly felt the room begin to spin.

Julie grabbed ahold of him saying, "Be careful, you've got a lump on your forehead the size of a boiled egg."

Zacharias began pawing at it and said, "Where did that come from."

Julie was still eyeing the lump on his forehead when she said,

"You took a hoof from that horse that Mexican man was riding when he chased us down. Hey Zachary, why did we run anyway? I mean, what freaked you out so bad, that you nearly tore my arm from its socket, hauling me after you like a rag doll?"

Zacharias answered, "It was because I recognized him!"

Julie said, "Recognized who? What are you talking about?"

"El demonio," said Zacharias. "The one Pancho Villa called Fierro! He's the demon from my nightmare! When I saw him in the flesh, I just lost it."

Julie said, "Back up a minute, did you just say Pancho Villa was there?"

Zacharias said, "Yeah, he was the one on the golden horse, that they kept calling, **Mi General** (*my general*)."

Julie retorted, "You mean the loud one?"

Zacharias said, "Yeah, the loud one, didn't you see him?"

Julie said, "That Mexican brute who threw me over his horse, kept my head pinned down with his knee, so I didn't see much, and understood even less, but I did see the two golden horse's, so does that mean that the other one was..."

But before she could finish, Zacharias interrupted saying, "Yes, it was my Bis-ABUELO! I tried to tell him he was my Abuelo, but....but heck…its even hard for me to believe, so how could he…I mean it's so twisted. Then I remembered thinking that I should tell him about the key, but I'm not even sure if I got the words out, before I passed out. Hey how long have we been here anyway?"

Julie said, "A couple of hours, they brought us in through those cellar doors over there, but I've tried them, there bolted shut from the outside. And another thing...."

But before she could finish, an ear-splitting explosion rattled the cellar doors, and dust seeped in through the cracks, Zacharias began coughing, but Julie, who had been prepared, had her shirt stretched up over her nose and mouth.

She looked straight into Zachary's eyes and said, "That's been getting closer and more frequent!"

Suddenly like a slap in the face, the presence of war invaded his consciousness, he became acutely aware of gunfire, the thundering of hooves, and shrieks of battle, everything seemingly taking place just outside the very walls that sheltered them. (Like the instant collapse of a house built of cards.) Everything now tumbled upon him. The sobering reality of what they had endured, invaded his mind, Blackie was gone! And who knew if he even made it back. He and Julie were stranded in a war not of their time. Pepé would never walk at his side again. And he had failed to make himself known to his Abuelo when the opportunity had arisen. In short .he had failed at every turn! What had ever made him think, that he could conduct himself as a man!

Then he began thinking that giving up wouldn't be so bad, not if he did it just this once! It's not like if he would create a habit of doing so; everything would be so much easier.

Then another explosion, this one had made a direct hit on the Hacienda; there was no doubt in Zacharias' mind about that. When he looked up and caught sight of Julie, only one word could describe the look on her face.... FEAR!

In that split second, he felt something shift with-in him, like a pendulum that had been frozen in time, and was now free to swing. Immediately he felt disgusted with himself, for having been more concerned about his own short-comings, rather than the well-being of his friends, and for pitying himself.

Here he mocked himself, I'll just give up this once; it won't become habit. HOW PATHETIC! How could he have allowed the seeds of a coward to germinate within him? Had he not learned any of his papi's lessons!

Then relief washed over him, for he knew, that if his papi had been here to witness, his seemingly absent altruistic principles, and ignoble behavior. It would have surely elicited shame, and deservedly so!

The realization that he had disillusioned himself about being a man was a hard pill to swallow. Then he thought, I may not be a man yet, but I'm certainly not a child! Here he leaned forward and took Julie's hand in his and said, "Don't worry, I'm not sure how yet, but I'm gonna get us out of this, I promise."

Julie was about to respond when they both froze, as they heard the latch on the cellar doors being tugged on from the outside.

Zacharias' instincts took over, he jumped to his feet and scanned the cellar for a weapon, his eyes came to rest on a pitchfork leaning up against the far wall; he made a mad dash for it and snatched it up with both hands. As he spun on his heels to face the stairs, he saw a pair of legs on the second step from the top, then another explosion caused the person to lose his footing, and come tumbling down head over heels in a cloud of dust and smoke.

Zacharias' only thoughts were for Julie's safety. He scrambled towards the foot of the stairs, knowing he would have the element of surprise on who he suspected to be the Demonio himself.

The cloud of dust and smoke was so thick, that if it hadn't been for the ray of light coming in from the open cellar doors, he wouldn't have been able to locate the stairs. As he approached, he heard Julie trying to stifle her coughing, ahead and to the left, he couldn't see, but sensed the brute, ahead and to his right.

He raised the pitchfork and was about to lunge, when Julie screamed, "ZACHARY NO, IT'S BLACKIE!"

Blackie had landed flat on his rear-end in a sitting position at the foot of the stairs, as the smoke cleared, Blackie realized Zacharias was hovering over him, pitchfork at the ready. For a moment, his eyes widened, then he simply reached up, grabbed his spectacles that had been teetering perilously from one ear, affixed them on his face, blinked twice, and said, "I see your still upset with me ole' chap."

Zacharias dropped the pitchfork, and he and Julie were atop of Blackie, hugging and pawing him as if they couldn't believe it was really him.

Blackie said, "Stop that you two. I feel like an old lost dog that's just come home after being lost for two weeks."

Even though Julie had tears in her eyes, she and Zacharias began giggling.

Blackie said, "Come on I mean it, I took quite a tumble you know, I could've broke something, come on let me up, I'M SERIOUS Right now!"

Both Zacharias and Julie began giggling harder.

As Zacharias attempted to pull Blackie to his feet, his arm came to rest on the wooden box strapped to his back, in the next two seconds that it took to get Blackie upright, Zacharias had made up his mind as to what they would do next.

He said, "Blackie, please tell me you still have the key?"

"Absolutely, I would have protected it with my life, if such a situation had arisen," said Blackie.

Zacharias said, "I wouldn't doubt that for a minute, you crazy Englishman!"

Blackie was grinning from ear to ear, as he extracted the key from his pocket and presented it to Zacharias.

Zacharias grabbed it, placed it around his neck and said, "This is the end of the road for us, forget the gold, forget everything, I'm not gonna...."

Blackie interrupted saying, "What do you mean the end of the road, we're so close, all we have to do is...."

Here Zacharias interrupted saying, "No! Up until now, I've made some poor decisions, that have put all of us in harm's way, I finally realized, that the loyalty and friendship that has grown between us, is the real treasure in life. You two have become like family to me, and I'm just not prepared to gamble with your lives any longer, not for any

111

amount of money."

The respect and admiration on Julie's face upon hearing this did not go unnoticed by Blackie.

Zacharias placed his hand on Blackie's shoulder and said, "We live to conquer another day, trust me my friend; this is the right thing to do."

Blackie stood silent a moment looking at Zacharias, then said, "Sometimes I get caught up in the moment, and can't see the forest for the trees, but your absolutely right ole' chap, we live to conquer another day. Now give me a hand with this thing, so we can get outta here!"

CHAPTER 13

As Zacharias began to untie the rope that had kept the wooden box secured on Blackie's back, he glanced over towards Julie and said, "I could use a hand over...., but his words stopped in mid-sentence as he noticed Julie's ridged posture, it was as if she was rooted to the ground, and the expression on her face, was that of sheer terror!

He twisted his neck around even further following her line of sight; it came to rest on the silhouette of the largest man Zacharias had ever seen.

The man seemed to engulf the entire staircase, and with the sun at his back, he appeared to be ten feet tall, the man wore a sombrero, and a bandolier crisscrossed his torso. He was clutching a large caliber rifle in his hands, and a pair of forty-fives hung at his waist sides.

Zacharias' heart leaped into his throat, for it seemed that he could smell the very stench of death that seeped out of the pores of this human war machine. Before he knew what he was doing, he had seized his pitchfork, and was lunging towards this silhouette of death, when another direct hit on the Hacienda, sent him sprawling to the ground at the foot of the stairs, as he raised his head, he glimpsed sight of the Mexican brute, leaping over him from the step he had been standing on.

Zacharias twisted over onto his back, trying to bring the pitchfork around into a defensive position, but he hadn't been quick enough, the jolt of the boot slamming down and pinning the pitchfork on to his chest, had knocked the wind out of him. He was furious with himself, for having allowed this Mexican brute to have bested him so easily, and was about to say so, when his vision cleared, and he came face to face with his Abuelo smiling down on him, then he immediately felt his Abuelo's body jerk, and heard him yelp..." **Aaahhhiiii!**" ("Ouucchhhh!")

That's when Zacharias noticed Blackie's arms wrapped around his Abuelo's leg and his teeth embedded into his thigh.

114

His Abuelo yelled out, "**Muchacho Salvaje' Malcriado, me vas a sacar el Pedazo!**" (*"You're going to tear out a chunk of my thigh. You! I've raised jungle boy!"*)

Zacharias yelled, "BLACKIE NO, IT'S MY ABUELO!"

Blackie immediately retreated with a look of shock on his face, he began to stammer out.... "Sorry...I'm...I'm sorry sir," as he retreated two more steps. His Abuelo was still pawing at his thigh, as he turned his attention back to Zacharias, again he grinned, and said, "**No hay duda que eres un Garcia hasta el hueso!**" (*"There's no doubt that you're a Garcia to the bone!"*)

He removed his foot, reached down and pulled Zacharias up by the scruff of the shoulder, and planted him on his feet.

Zacharias was experiencing an array of emotions, shock; being the vanguard, he could only summon the words, "**Eres, eres mi Bis-Abuelo.**" (*"You're... you're my great grandfather."*)

This mountain of a man that was his Abuelo said, "**Ya lo se hijo, la primera vez que nos encontramos, aunque tenias el parecido a mi genté, no te lo crei, despues, cuando mencionasté la llave (aqui su Abuelo toca la llave colgando alrededor del cuello de Zacharias, con sus dedos, como asegurandosé, que por cierto, lo que estaba viendo, realmenté estaba pasando) me pusisté a pensar, pero no hubo tiempo para contemplar las posibilidades. Como dice' mi**

General Villa,'La Revolucion, no espera a ninguno! Pero por Los santos, no pudé sacar tú imagen de mi menté, y por eso me devolvi, cuando iba llegando, espié este Puercoespin con el pelo rojo, tratando de abrir las puertas del sotano. Es cuando vi el Trasmigrador Osmosis Celestial C.O.T. de los Teotihuacanos, atras de su espalda. Cuando empezé ha bajar los escalones, tenias el Puercoespin al punto de la horquilla, Pensaba que te lo ibias a hechar al plato, hasta que mé di cuenta que era tú amigo." (*"I'm already aware of that son, after our first encounter, even after noticing the resemblance, I did not believe you. Later when you mentioned the key (here, he touched the key hanging around Zacharias' neck with his fingers, as if reassuring himself, that what he was seeing was in fact real) you made me pause and think, but there was no time to contemplate the possibilities. Like my general Pancho Villa says, ('the revolution awaits no man!') but for the saints, I could not get your image out of my mind, and that's why I returned. As I approached the hacienda, I spied that red-headed porcupine trying to breach the cellar doors. That's when I saw the teotihuacanos C.O.T. strapped to his back. As I descended the stairs, I saw you at the verge of running your pitchfork through the porcupine, I thought you were about to serve him up on a platter, until I realized he was your friend."*)

It was at this moment that Zacharias felt the full impact of everything he, Blackie, and Julie had faced; in truth, it felt as if they had been on this journey for a month, then to finally be standing here in front of his Abuelo was overwhelming.

Zacharias took two steps forward and wrapped his arms around his Abuelo's waist, digging his face into his ribs. He felt his Abuelo wince and release a rush of air.

Then his Abuelo embraced him and said, **"Escuchamé hijo, ser el encargado de la llave, no es solamenté un privilegio, pero una mision de vida, puedé ser una bendicion O una maldicion. Que nunca se te olvidé, que solamenté se debe usar, para el bienestar y avanzamiento de la humanidad, si deliberadamenté se usa por maldad, Los implicados, sufriran la maldicion de los que construyeron las piramides, por su puesto, era el pacto que hicieron los Teotihuacanos, con los hermanos celestiales. Ellos fueron los que ingeniaron el C.O.T.. Hijo, como deseo tener mas tiempo, tengo muchas cosas que contarte'....Ah, primeramenté, has encontrado el oro?"** (*"Son listen to me, being the keeper of the key, is not only a privilege, but a life's mission, it can be a blessing and a curse, never forget that it should only be used for the well-being and advancement of humanity, if it is ever deliberately used for evil, those involved, will suffer the wrath or curse of the pyramid builders, for it was the Teotihuacan people, and their pact with the celestial brothers whom engineered the C.O.T. Son, how I wish I had more time, I have so many things to tell you, ah first of all, have you located the gold yet?"*)

Zacharias responded, "**No....no sabiamos donde buscar, ni estabamos seguros si en verdad existia. Se le aparecio una sonrisa a su Abuelo, y dijo, por su puesto, que si existé, y porque tienes el C.O.T., eso mé dicé, que casi estabas arriba del oro, y ni cuenta te disté.**

Cuando vuelvas a la mansion, adentro de la chimenea, a la mano derecha, como cuatro pies de altura, encuentras la Palanca que te revelara la herencia tuya, y la de tú familia.

Aqui su Abuelo lo mira directo en sus ojos, y dicé, Pero lo que es de mas gran importancia, eres tú, la llave te escogio a ti, ahora tu' eres el encargado, aunque no comprendo las razones, Parece' que le destino de los tres esta entre lazado, y ahi se tendra que quedar.

Hijo, nunca dejes a nadie saber de la llave 0 su proposito, hacer esto seria catastrofico, Solamente ustedes tres tendran el Conocimiento.

Hijo, simpre' recuerda que contigo cargas la fe y fuerza de tús antepasados."

("No, we didn't know where to look, or even if it really existed." A grin shown on his Abuelo's face as he said, "It most certainly does exist, and seeing that you have the C.O.T. in your possession, means that you were nearly on top of it, and didn't know it.

When you return to the mansion, inside the fireplace, to the right hand side, about four feet high, is a lever that will reveal yours, and your families inheritance."

Here his Abuelo looks him straight in the eyes and says, "But what's of greater importance is you, the key chose you, you are the keeper now, for reasons that I do not fully understand, it appears that all three of your destinies are intertwined, and there it must stay.

Son, never allow anyone outside your circle of three, to gain knowledge of the key, or its purpose, to do so, could be catastrophic. Son, always remember, that you carry with you all the trust and strength of your ancestors.")

Somewhere above them another canon blast hits home, his Abuelo says with some urgency, **"Hijo, llama la Revolucion, y ustedes tres se tendran que ir."** (*"Son, the Revolution calls, and you three must be going."*)

Upon hearing this, Zacharias pulled out of their embrace, as he did so, he felt a dampness on his face, he instinctively pawed at it, his hand came away smeared in blood, for a moment he was shocked and confused, then he saw his Abuelos entire left side and midsection, drenched in blood.

Zacharias shouted, **"Abuelo estas Sangrando!"** (*"Abuelo you're bleeding!"*)

His Abuelo says, "**Si hijo, ya lo se, no te apures, se mira peor de lo que es.**" ("*Yes son, I'm already aware, don't worry yourself, it appears worse than it is.*")

Here another explosion rocks the Hacienda. His Abuelo turns and makes for the foot of the stairs saying, "**Me llama la Revolucion!**" ("*The revolution is calling!*")

Zacharias in a state of indecision looks over at Blackie and Julie; his feet had already started forward, before he was even aware he had made a decision. He grasps his Abuelo around the waist and says, "**Abuelo, te tengo que decir algo muy importanté, en la historia de esta fecha, es cuando tú....**"

Aqui su Abuelo lo interrumpio, "No mijo, no quiero saber, pero si te quiero dejar con un consejo. Pararté de pie,y pelear por justicia y tus creencias, es la cosa mas digna y honorablé, que un hombre' puede hacer en su vida.

Mijo, todo lo que representa Mexico.

La batalla contra la opression, La lucha contra el hambre!

La justicia por la igualdad!

el corazon y el espiritud, que nunca se da por vencido, de toda la genté pobré, de mi Mexico Querido.

(Todo esto es la revolucion!) y haber participado en esta lucha, hacido una bendicion, y un honor."

(Aqui se agacha, y poné sus manos arriba de los hombros de Zacharias y dicé)

"Un hombre' siempre' se poné de pie por sus creencias, sin mirar las consecuencias.

Antes de irme, seria mi honor, saber tú verdadero nombré."

Zacharias tranca ojos con su Abuelo y dicé,

"Me llamo como usted Abuelito (aqui por la primera vez, usando el titulo de su Abuelo con compassion sincera) me llamo Zacharias Garcia."

Se le formo un nudo en la garganta a su Abuelito, empezo a enderezarsé, hasta que quedo a su estatura.

Sin que se diera cuenta, se le lleno el pecho con orgullo, y una sonrisa aparecio.

En el momento antes que su Abuelito se volteo a irse, Zacharias estaba seguro que miro, que se le habia escapado una lagrima, pero cuando menos acordo, ya habia salido su Abuelito del sotano, y es cuando escucho el galopar de un Caballo, y el grito que solto su Abuelito" (VIVA LA REVOLUCION!)"

En ese momento, Zacharias sabia en su corazon, que iban a ser las ultimas palabras que iba escuchar de su Abuelito.

(*"Abuelo, I have something very important to tell you, today on this very date in history, is when you...,"*)

Here his Abuelo interrupts him, "No my son, I don't want to know, but I do wish to impart upon you some advise.

Always stand up and fight for your beliefs, and also for justice, this is the most worthy, and honorable thing a man can do with his life.

My son, everything that represents Mexico, the battle against oppression, the fight against hunger, seeking justice in equality, and the never wavering, poor man's heart and spirit, in my beloved Mexico....(All of this is the revolution!)

And to have been blessed, to have been allowed to participate in its struggle for reformation, has been nothing less than an honor."

(Here he leans over and puts his hands atop Zacharias' shoulders and says "A man always stands up for his beliefs, no matter the consequences. Before I depart, allow me the honor of knowing your given name?"

Zacharias locks eyes with his Abuelo and says, "I'm your name sake Abuelito (Here for the first time using his Abuelo's title with sincere compassion). My name is Zacharias Garcia."

Jerry Garcia

A lump begins to form in his Abuelo's throat, as he straightens up to his full height, without having been aware of it, his breast had filled with pride, and a smile shown on his face.

In that last moment before his Abuelito turns to leave, Zacharias could have sworn he'd seen a tear trickle out of his eye.

In the next moment, his Abuelito was gone out the cellar doors. What followed was the thundering of hoof, and the shout that escaped his abuelo's lips...("VIVA LA REVOLUCION!")

In that instant, Zacharias' heart told him, that these would be the last words he would ever hear from his Abuelito.)

Key of Destiny

CHAPTER 14

Viva la revolucion....was still ringing in Zacharias' ears, when another explosion rocked the very foundations of the Hacienda.

Blackie jerked him around by the shoulder saying, "We have to go, we have to go now!"

Zacharias sprang into action helping Blackie remove the remaining rope from around the C.O.T.

Blackie kept ahold of it while Zacharias fumbled with the cylinders, when he was done it read, September 16, 2014 Denver

Colorado, U. S .A. Zacharias removed the key from around his neck, inserted it and said, "All right grab ahold."

When all three had a firm grip on the C.O.T. he turned the key.

The last thing they saw as they began to spin was the cellar doors explode, but they never heard a sound, then darkness, and the showering of stars, but this time it felt different, Zacharias felt as if he was being watched.

The realization, that existence was farther beyond then what he could ever have imagined, was all at once exciting, and frightening, but he also felt a connection, or cycle of eternity (a oneness in purpose).

A germination of understanding began to develop deep within him.

The realization that this miracle bestowed upon him should be used for the discovery of ancient wisdom and forgotten knowledge, in order for him to best serve humanity. His next thoughts were of why? Why had his bloodline been chosen for such a monumental and noble endeavor? Could it be that he....

The impact of the marble floor in the sacred chamber brought him outta his musings, the room was in shambles, but the ever present aroma of tobacco and pecans was unmistakable.

He began first pawing at Julie, then at Blackie saying, "Are you okay? Are either of you guys hurt?"

Julie said, "I'm a little dizzy, but other than that, I think I'm okay."

Blackie looked around and said, "YES, WE'RE BACK!"

The thought that it had all been a dream, flashed in Julie's brain, but dissipated just as quickly, as her vision focused in on first Blackie, then Zachary.

Both their faces were smeared in black smudge from the smoke, and they were covered from head to toe in dirt.

She blurted out, "You two are filthy!"

Blackie and Zacharias both looked at her and began giggling.

Julie said, "What.... what are you guys laughing at?"

Blackie said, "Just be thankful there's not a mirror in here."

This brought another round of giggling from the both of them. Blackie caught sight of the fireplace, and his expression turned serious, he pointed at it with his right forefinger, turned to Zach and said, "Should we have a look?"

Following the direction of Blackie's out-stretched finger, Zacharias' line of sight came to rest on the fireplace, without saying a word, he began making his way towards it, with Blackie at his side, and Julie bringing up the rear, self-consciously pawing at her hair; an effort in futility as it turned out.

As they approached, Blackie caught sight of a flashlight under one of the upturned chairs, he reached down, picked it up and pushed the button, nothing happened, he banged it against his thigh and it came to life.

As he turned towards the fireplace, he noticed Zach was already on top of the stepping stone, and was reaching down to help Julie up, he yelled out, "Hey, wait for me!"

As they entered the fireplace, Blackie shone the beam of light on the back wall, it was partitioned in three sections, each section was constructed of sheet metal that was about four feet in width, and about six feet in height.

Zacharias having made his way to the far right corner said, "Hey Blackie, give me some light over here."

Blackie turned illuminating the entire corner, right above Zacharias' head, was an iron spike, like the ones used to nail down railroad ties, he grabbed ahold with his right hand and pulled downward, it didn't budge, he grabbed ahold with both hands and suspended himself from it, applying the weight of his entire body, and still it wouldn't give.

Blackie brought the flashlight closer and said, "Look Zach, there's an iron ring in-laid around the base. That spike isn't gonna shift up or down.

Zacharias stood back and looked at it a moment, then reached up and placed the heel of his palm against the head of the spike, and pushed in, it was stiff, but slowly the spike sunk in flush with the wall, you could hear what sounded like a gear catch within, and in the next second, the partition on the right, raised straight up into the ceiling.

Zacharias took two steps forward, Blackie shuffled over standing shoulder to shoulder with him, both were jostled aside, as Julie began wriggling her body in-between them, Blackie gave Julie a sideways menacing glance, but after seeing the determination on her face, relinquished the option to voice his opinion. When he regained his composure, he brought the flashlight up illuminating the esoteric enclave.

All three stood staring, as if in disbelief, of what they were in fact seeing.

Centered in the middle of the room, were three wooden pallets, the first, was stacked about three feet high with golden bricks.

The second was stacked just as high, with wooden crates filled with odd shaped golden nuggets.

The third had several bulging canvas sacks, some were frayed at the ends, and you could see where fine gold dust had seeped out.

Julie blurted out, "ZACHARY, YOU'RE RICH!"

Zacharias, who was staring at the gold, didn't utter a word.

Blackie interjected saying, "I hope you allow this moment to serve as an indelible imprint in your memory, as to the constant thread of connection, between past, and present. We must never underestimate the long reaching arm of history."

He spreads out his arms towards the gold and says, "It can obviously bestow miracles, but it can also just as easily, deliver a crippling blow. In this case, the stars were aligned correctly, or we garnered auspicious favor with the God's, whatever your beliefs, fortune has certainly smiled upon us, I speak not of the gold, but of our health, and safe return."

Zacharias was still staring at the gold, but the expression conveyed on his face, was that of sadness. Then in a low voice, almost as if to himself he said, "But what good is this?"

He reaches up and clasps the key dangling around his neck and says, "WHAT GOOD WAS THIS FREAKING KEY FOR, IF I WASN'T ABLE TO SAVE MY ABUELO?"

Blackie interjected saying, "Don't be so hard on yourself, nothing you would have said, or done, would have changed his mind. He was fully aware of his fate, he chose to sacrifice himself for his country, to him the Revolution was larger than any one life, no matter what the consequences, men of that caliber and conviction, never compromise their morals, (Here Blackie places his hand on Zach's shoulder and says, "And that ole' chap, is what they call, TRUE CHARACTER!"

Julie said, "He fought for his beloved Mexico, he fought for humanity, and like Pepé , he died a hero's death, neither one, would of had it any other way."

Zacharias stood silent absorbing what Blackie and Julie had said, as his gaze came to rest on what appeared to be a parchment of paper sticking up out of one of the canvas sacks. Zacharias pointed and said, "Hey what's that?"

All three moved in tandem towards the canvas sack.

Zacharias reached out and grabbed it; it had the double fold of a conventional letter.

Blackie had his flashlight pointed directly at it.

Zacharias flipped it over; staring back at them was a wax seal, with a skeleton key impression.

Zacharias broke the seal, the parchment crinkled as he opened it, he began to read aloud.

Yo Zacharias Garcia:

Capitan en las fuerzas Revolucionarias de mi Mexico Querido.

Bajo el encargo de PANCHO VILLA, en este' 25, dia de Octubre' Mil Novecientos Diez.

Le dejo a mi hijo JUAN GARCIA, y ha su primer nacido

hijo, y el primer nacido hijo del, y hasta que siga.

Lo hago en esperanzas, que continuen adiciones y mejorias en nuestra Mansion, que he ayudado hacer con mis propias manos. Deseo que se quedé en la familia Para siempré.

Muchas veces en la Vida de un hombre. Uno se da Cuenta que el mayor Tesoro que se adquiere, no Viene del dinero, sino del Cariño de los amigos y la familia.

Te dejo Con las esperanzas, que nunca alejes tu derecho humano de pararté a pelear—

POR LO QUE ES JUSTO!

POR TUS CREENCIAS!

-Y- POR Tú GENTÉ!

POSTDATA:

Para el encargado

Siempre estaremos Contigo.

El destino no esta escrito en Piedra, lo podras doblar y torcer, menos cortar.

Todo lo que te pase, te pasa en todas dimensiones.

Jerry Garcia

QUE VIAJEN LOS DIOSES CONTIGO!

To Zacharias Garcia:

Captain in my beloved Mexico's revolutionary forces, under the command of Pancho Villa, on this 25, day of October, nineteen ten.

Here by leave this treasure of gold, to my son, Juan Garcia, and to his first born son, and to his first born son, and so on. I do so in hopes that they will continue improvements, and or additions to this mansion that I myself had a hand in building. It is my wish that it stay in the family forever.

More often than not, it is in the suns descent of a man's life, that he realizes, the greatest treasure one can acquire, does not come in monetary form, but lies within the bosom, of his family and friends.

I leave you in hopes, that you never alienate your human right, to stand up and fight.

For what's just!

For your beliefs!

And for your loved ones!

Post Scriptum:

To the Keeper,

We are always with you. Destiny, is not written in stone, you may bend and twist, just be certain not to sever. Everything that happens to you happens in every dimension. May the Gods journey with you.

When he was done reading his Abuelo's letter, he looked up as if to the heavens and said, "At first, I was angry with myself, because I wasn't able to save you," as he looks directly at Blackie and Julie he says. "But after listening to my friends, they made me realize, that even if I could have, you would have never allowed it. You practiced what you preached, you never wavered in protecting your Family, your Country, or what was just. You upheld your beliefs unto your last breath, and even though I'm still a boy. Because of you Abuelito, I understand the qualities that mark the true measure of a man. I don't know yet what I'm supposed to do, or why? I hope that when the time comes, I am able to conduct myself with half the wisdom and courage you have shown me."

He couldn't have said when, because he hadn't noticed it until this very moment, but Blackie's right hand was on his left shoulder, and Julie had clasped his right hand in hers.

With quivering lip, he continued, **"Tu' espiritud siempre' vivira en mi corazon, te amo Abuelito; Vaya Con Dios!"** (*Your spirit will forever live within my heart, I love you Abuelito; go with God!*).

CHAPTER FIFTEEN

Zacharias said, "I understand that I couldn't alter my Abuelo's destiny, not because it wasn't possible, but because he wouldn't allow it, but I still don't get it? I mean, I know we found the gold, and that that means we can afford to keep the mansion and all, but is that it? I mean what was all that stuff about humanity, and a life's mission? **Por los Santos** (*for the saints*) I have more questions now then when we started."

Julie said, "Hey guys, there's something else that's been bothering me, I didn't really wanna bring it up, because I'm still not sure, or, I mean, it could have just been me. But when we came back, I felt like someone, or something was watching us as we traveled, but I...."

Before she could finish, Zacharias jerked her around by the arm and spat-out, "ME TOO!"

Blackie yelled out, "ME TOO! I thought I was just being paranoid."

Julie said, "What does it mean? I mean, what could it have been?"

All three simultaneously felt the goose flesh rise on their arms; Julie wriggled her body as the goose flesh traveled up her spine to her neck.

Zacharias was the first one to regain his composure, knowing that Julie was experiencing the fear that he had just felt, said, "Okay, hold on a minute; let's not get ahead of ourselves."

Blackie interrupted saying, "Zach's right. I mean, we should first evaluate what we know."

Julie out of sheer anxiety, blurted out, "And what the heck is that Blackwood, we don't know anything!"

All three stood silent a moment, then Blackie continued, "Didn't your Obwaylo say that the Teotihuacan people had a hand in building the C.O.T.? My knowledge on the Teotihuacan people, is sketchy at best, do you know anything about them Zach?"

"Opinions differ, not a lot is known about them," said Zacharias. "I mean, we know they existed from about 200 B.C. to about 650 A.D. and that during this time, they built the largest city in what is today known as the Americas. What's more amazing, is that with primitive tools, and what is believed of today as inferior knowledge, they were able to build, which still stands until this day, one of the greatest wonders of the world, The Pyramid of the Sun. This spectacular Pyramid was the epicenter of religious worship, several smaller Pyramids, Temples, and palaces that surround the great Pyramid of the Sun, have also been unearthed, along with hundreds of residential dwellings and businesses.

By all accounts, this Metropolis, boasted easily over a hundred thousand, and possibly even up towards a quarter of a million people, but the most perplexing aspect, as my papi always says, is that it seems that the Teotihuacan people, inexplicably simply vanished overnight.

Modern excavations haven't revealed any large scale annihilations of buildings, and there have been minimal signs of buildings being ravaged by battle, nor have there been any proven signs of natural catastrophe.

It appears as if the Teotihuacan people collectively deserted their Metropolis overnight."

"YOU'RE KIDDING ME," said Julie. "An entire race simply vanishes.... never to be heard from again. That's just not possible!"

"I feel the same way," said Zacharias. "But that doesn't change the fact, that as far as history is concerned, the Teotihuacan people met an abrupt end. No one knows for sure what happened back then, there's several different theories, Deforestation, Soil Erosion, Endemic Disease, there's even an Alien Theory."

Blackie interrupted saying, "That brings me to my second question. Who were these celestial brothers? Your Obwaylo said, that the Teotihuacan people made a pact with these brothers, if I remember correctly, he said these brothers drew up the blue prints, or, engineered it, to use your Obwaylo's words, which makes perfect sense, because he called it the Celestial Osmosis Transmigrater, or C.O.T. Celestial being the operative word, which means, of the heavens, or of the stars. If we take all of this into account, along with our collective response to being watched on our return trip, one can only surmise..."

But before he could finish, Julie had jumped over and squared-up face to face with Blackie yelling at the top of her lungs, "ARE YOU OUTTA YOU'RE FREAKING MIND, WILLIAM BLACKWOOD MORGAN?? YOU'VE FINALLY DONE IT!! YOU'VE GONE INSANE!"

Zacharias jumped in-between them facing Julie saying, "Calm

down Julie, it's okay....what's wrong with you?"

Julie looked square into Zacharias' eyes and said, "Zachary, Don't you get it? Don't you understand what he was about to say? He's concocted some cockamamie story to try and scare us!"

Blackie blurted-out, "I HAVE NOT!"

Julie retorted, "YES YOU HAVE! WHO IN THEIR RIGHT MIND, BELIEVES IN, ALIENS!!! NOW DO YOU GET IT ZACHARY??? ALIENS FOR HEAVEN'S SAKE!"

Zacharias had been trying to piece all of this together ever since they had returned and at this moment he realized that somewhere in the back of his mind, he had been drawing the same conclusions. But, to have heard Julie's bold declaration out loud, had literally stunned him.

Julie continued, "ALIENS!! ALIENS! THAT'S WHAT YOU'RE SAYING, ISN'T IT BLACKWOOD?"

Blackie said, "I didn't mean to scare you, but we have to face the facts as they are; believe me, my conclusion is not whimsical. I've exhausted every avenue, to try and disprove what I feel in my gut to be true; it's the only logical explanation."

Julie said, "LOGICAL....LOGICAL!!! WHO DO YOU THINK YOU ARE? SPOCK?"

Zacharias said, "Okay stop, both of you, stop it." He looks over at Blackie and says, "Blackie, are you absolutely sure about this?"

Without skipping a beat Blackie says, "Of course not! It's just a guess, but it's my best educated guess."

All three stood silently digesting what had been said.

Blackie continued, "What I suspect to be true, in the end, is simply a theory. There's just no way to be certain, and at this point, I have more questions than answers. Like you Zach; how do you fit into the equation? Or your Obwaylo, for that matter? And who was the keeper before him?"

Zacharias said, "I can think of one way of finding out."

Julie said, "OH MY GOD! NOT JUST ONE, BUT TWO LUNATICS! Why is it that I have to be the only sane person in the room, when all three of us are together?"

Blackie chuckled and said, "She's absolutely right you know. If you're saying, what I think you're saying, Zach it's just too dangerous. Listen to me; we were lucky to have escaped with our lives. If those two Mexican boys would have been any older, we would have been done for. If we would have run into any other regiment, other than your Obwaylo's, we would have been done for. Are you kidding me! We were in the mists, of the Mexican revolution for Christ sake! If our exposure would have been any greater, one or all of us could have taken a stray bullet. I'm just saying, we were bloody lucky this time. It was a fluke. I don't know, maybe the stars were aligned correctly, or the gods showed compassion on our soles, or...."

Zacharias interrupts saying, "Or....it was destiny!"

Julie stares directly at Zacharias and says, "OH MY GOD! We're going back, aren't we?"

A smile flashed across Zacharias' face, then he shrugged his shoulders and said, "You never know."

Key of Destiny

ABOUT THE AUTHOR

Mr. Garcia was born in Ballinger, Texas. He comes from a family of migrant workers and is the youngest of eleven children. Shortly after his birth, his family settled in Dayton, Oregon.

Mr. Garcia is currently laying the ground work for the sequel to *Key of Destiny*.

Key of Destiny